Where Heroes Hide

✹

FOR ALL THE MEN AND WOMEN WHO SERVED
IN THE ARMED FORCES DURING WORLD WAR II—
EACH ONE A HERO. MAY WE ALWAYS REMEMBER
THEIR SACRIFICE AND COURAGE.

✹

Where Heroes Hide

Chapter One

Summer vacation. I started the countdown as soon as my teacher, Miss Kane, tore May off the calendar. At three o'clock on that last day of classes in June, I raced out of Grove Street School as if my pants were on fire. Each minute would matter. I'd stretch out the days like soft bubble gum.

That first morning I got up early and joined my dad and my sister, Linda, for breakfast in the kitchen. Mom had just put a pile of Aunt Jemima pancakes on the table.

"Look who's here!" Linda said. Linda worked first shift at Mansfield-Davis Mill, like my dad. Dad was a foreman in the spinning department at the yarn mill, but Linda worked in the office.

She was a secretary—her first real job after graduating from high school that May.

"What are you doing up?" Dad asked. "No school today, remember?"

"My friends are coming over early."

"Hmm . . . which friends?"

"Bobby . . ."

"Bobby and?"

I sighed. I knew Dad would be mad. Bobby and Lenny.

Lenny-with-the-leg. That's what some people called him. Not me, though. Lenny and I had been friends since first grade. One day he was sitting behind me at school, snapping my suspenders and hollering out the answer when it was my turn, and the next day he was absent. And the next day. And the next week. His mother said he must have caught a virus. That's what everyone thought until the doctor gave Lenny's parents the bad news. Polio. Lenny had polio. From time to time Lenny's mother would phone my mother with updates on his condition.

"That poor woman just cries her heart out," Mom said, "and sometimes I just cry along with her. I don't know what they're going to do about those hospital bills. Lenny's father doesn't make all that much money selling life insurance. Life insurance—isn't that a twisted thought! Who can be sure about anything?"

I sure missed Lenny. There was a classroom full of kids, but it was lonesome without him. Lenny went through some tough times for a couple of years. He stayed in the hospital for months.

"Children's ward. Breaks my heart to even think of a place like that," Mom said. "I sure hope that little guy makes it."

And he did. He pulled through. But now he wore a heavy metal brace on his right leg, and he had an odd, hitch-along walk, his leg sticking out at an angle. After he'd been tutored at home, this had been his first year back in school.

"Bobby and Lenny," I answered.

"Lenny? That polio kid?" Dad shouted. "I told you, I don't want you hanging around with him! Bad enough he's right there in school with the rest of you kids! I don't want you hanging around with him!"

"Now, Joe," Mom said. "It's perfectly safe. He's not contagious. I've told you that. And Junior's all set. He's had his polio shot. Dr. Lewis said there's nothing to worry about."

I remembered the day Dr. Lewis came to our school to give us our Salk vaccine. Dr. Lewis's daughter Nancy was in my class. We were all lined up, and Nancy was right in front of me. When her father swabbed her arm with alcohol, Nancy pulled away.

"I don't want a shot!" she yelled. "It's going to hurt! It's going to hurt!"

"Now, Nancy, you've had shots before. You're a big girl. You know it will sting for only a second," her father said.

"No, no!" She was crying, wailing.

"Nancy!" Dr. Lewis said. "Stop carrying on! You're scaring the other kids."

Well, that was true. I gulped. My legs were shaking a little, and I was starting to sweat, too.

"Stop! Stop!" Nancy cried. "I'm going to faint! I'm going to faint!"

Dr. Lewis grabbed her arm and stuck in the needle. "There. You didn't faint. It's all over— until I see you at home tonight!" Then he called, "Next? Hi, Junior!"

Gulp.

"Junior's all set," Mom was telling Dad.

"I know what I know, Carol! It's 1956, and the

town still hasn't reopened the swimming pool at the playground because of those polio germs. I know about polio!" Dad said. "A little sore throat, a fever, a few aches and pains, and the next thing you know Junior can't walk. Maybe goes in an iron lung—can't even breathe!"

"But, Dad," Linda said. "President Roosevelt had polio. You liked him. Give Lenny a break."

"And who asked you for your two cents? You just sit there and keep quiet." Turning back to me, Dad said, "I don't want you hanging around with that kid. You hear?"

I wished Dad would leave me and Lenny alone. Didn't he know how mixed-up he made me feel? He was asking me to choose—him or Lenny. And I didn't like making him mad. He got mad enough about other things.

"We hear you," Mom said. "We hear you." She moved behind Dad's chair and winked at me. "Better watch the time, Joe. It's getting late. You, too, Linda."

"Yes. I'm leaving now." Linda grabbed her purse from the back of the chair. "Oh, and I'm not eating supper tonight, Mom. I have a date with Roger."

"Roger! Hmph! What do you see in that good-for-nothing?" Dad said. "A pinsetter at the bowling alley!"

I had to agree with Dad on that one. A couple of days before, I'd come into the house to get my baseball cards, and I heard Linda on the phone near the hall stairs.

"He's so proud of that car, you know. It's like it's his whole life!"

She was talking to her friend Rita about Roger's brand-new red-and-white '56 Chevy. It was some car all right. When the streetlights hit all that chrome, it turned night into day. Linda's back was to me, and she didn't know I was there. She was talking about Roger—I had to hear this! I slipped back into the living room.

"Promise you won't tell a soul, Rita. Oh, it's so embarrassing. Promise. Whenever Roger and I go out, I have to pay for everything. . . . I know. I know. But he's always broke because of his car payments."

She sounded so miserable, I almost felt bad about eavesdropping.

"And there's something else," she went on. "Whenever we go to Debby's Donut Drive-in, we have to get out of the car and eat outside. Why? He doesn't want crumbs in the car! It's so embarrassing! I know. I know. And one time at Hamburger Heaven I spilled a little soda on the dashboard, and he went wild."

✻ ✻ ✻

"I don't know how he can afford that fancy car of his," Dad was saying. "A pinsetter at the bowling alley!"

"Daddy, I told you. Roger's going to the community college this fall," Linda said.

"Yeah, and pigs'll whistle!" Dad yelled after her.

"Don't worry, Joe. She's a smart girl," Mom said. "She'll soon see the light of day. She's a lot like me—she has a mind of her own."

Chapter Two

After Linda and Dad left, Mom sat down at the table to have her breakfast.

"Is it true what Dad said?" I asked her. "Could I still get polio? From Lenny?"

"No, you can't. Dr. Lewis said Lenny isn't contagious. Dad's being overly cautious. He's like a lot of other people who don't really understand about polio."

"Well, Dad scares me when he talks about me getting sick."

"Don't be scared, honey." Mom patted my hand. "It may take time, but somehow we'll convince him that it's safe for you to be with Lenny."

I hoped Dad would be in a better mood when

he came home from work that night. I was trying to get up the courage to talk to him again about a bike. Now that my other friend, Bobby, had a nifty blue Raleigh to cruise around on, I wanted a bike of my own really bad.

Bobby and I were Junior Patrol crossing guards at our school last year. We each wore a badge, and everyone had to obey us at the crosswalk in front of the school. When a bunch of kids gathered, Bobby and I would blow our whistles and the cars would stop. Then we'd step off the curb and hold out our safety flags and allow the kids to cross. I liked how the kids looked up to us. No one made fun of Bobby, even though he talked funny. He didn't say *r*'s or *l*'s. When he said his name, Robert, it sounded like "Wobbit."

Bobby and I went to the citywide Junior Patrol Picnic at the end of the year. It was a reward for being responsible. We got a whole day out of school! We went to a park and had hot dogs and soda and ran relay races and played ball. At the end of the afternoon, there was a raffle for a bicycle—and Bobby won it! Bobby probably would never have gotten a bike otherwise. His mother was a waitress at the coffee shop, and there wasn't any money for things like bicycles. A man from the newspaper took Bobby's picture and everything. You should have seen Bobby grinning, standing next to that shiny blue Raleigh.

My dad had promised me one for my eleventh birthday, in October, but, gee, that was a long way off.

"Please, Dad? Please?" I had begged. "I need a bike this summer. I have half the money saved up from Christmas and from chores. Couldn't you just lend me the other half?"

"What kind of talk is that?" Dad asked. "Nobody gives me free money. You'll wait till your birthday, or you'll just have to save your allowance and earn the rest yourself. It'll give you something to do this summer."

Work! I bet he'd have gotten me a job at the mill if he could have! I was a kid—I just wanted to have fun. Dad didn't understand about fun. He never understood about anything. Maybe I'd better forget about asking him again. Whining would get me nowhere. He wouldn't put up with that.

I'd told Lenny and Bobby what my dad had said about earning money this summer.

"Mowing lawns maybe," I suggested.

"Hey, we could all get jobs this summer!"

Lenny said. "We could all make a lot of money and get rich!"

"Sounds good to me," Bobby said.

"But *you* don't have to save for a bike. You already have one," I said. I glanced at Lenny. I hoped he wasn't feeling bad knowing he couldn't ride a bike.

"Well, I could save for something else," Bobby said.

"What?"

"A raft!" Lenny said. "I've always wanted a raft. I can see myself now, paddling my raft on the pond. Taking the day off from everything, floating in the middle of the pond, catching a whole bucket of fish."

"Yeah," said Bobby. "Me, too. Hey, you and I could save up together for the raft."

"We could get one of those four-man rafts. It'd give me extra room for my leg, and Junior could ride in it with us, too."

Now, I thought this was a pretty nice thing for Lenny to say.

"I accept!" I said.

"Only if you let me ride your bike," Lenny said.

"What?"

"Just kidding!"

I blushed. Lenny was okay. Why couldn't Dad see that? And those mean kids who called him names? When people made fun of Lenny, I could see tears burning red in his eyes. Maybe that's why sometimes he acted wild, like he was all cranked up or something. Maybe those burning red eyes got tired of holding back.

I couldn't help feeling guilty about getting a bike. Bobby, Lenny, and I always did everything together. Bobby and I would have bikes, and Lenny would be left out.

"Mom, do you think it's wrong for me to want a bike when my best friend Lenny can't have one, too?"

Mom gave me a hug. "No, Junior, it's not wrong. If you had a leg brace, and Lenny didn't, would you be mad at him if he wanted a bike?"

"No," I said.

"You'd want him to have fun, and he wants you to have fun, too. I'm sure there are times when Lenny feels bad about his leg, but he's full of spunk. Things will work out for him. Maybe someday his leg will get better and he won't have to wear the brace anymore. Who knows? It's very nice of you to think about your friend's feelings, but it's not wrong for you to want a bike."

There was a rap at the screen door.

"Bobby!" I said.

"Another early bird! Come on in," Mom called. "Got some extra pancakes here. Come on in."

Bobby sat in Linda's empty chair.

"Bobby, where's your bike?" I asked.

"It's no fun if you and Lenny can't ride with me. I didn't bring it." Only it sounded like "bwing."

"So what do you think?" Bobby asked. "Are you still going to mow lawns this summer?"

"What's this about lawns?" Mom asked.

"Maybe."

"Well, why don't you ask nice Mrs. Witowicz next door to hire you. She tries to take care of her yard herself, but she's getting too old."

"Aw, Mom," I said. "She's got that haunted shed in her yard. I told you about the noises I hear at night. There's something out there—or in there."

For a while now I'd been hearing awful noises coming from that shed. At first I'd thought it was Mrs. Witowicz's cat fighting with another cat. Then it seemed more like a coyote howling. I'd sat peering out my bedroom window many nights, unable to sleep. Maybe Mom was right. Maybe it was my imagination running away with me, but it sure was a wild sound—like something in pain.

"Stop that nonsense right now," Mom said. "That's just Mrs. Witowicz. She goes out there sometimes at night and sits in the shed. Her Benny's shed."

Benny was her husband, and he died several months ago. Mom said Mrs. Witowicz was missing her Benny, and that she went out to the shed when she was feeling sad and lonely.

"Benny built that shed and kept all his garden tools there. They're probably still in there. The poor old woman sits in there and cries for her husband. That's all you hear."

If that was supposed to settle me down, it sure didn't.

"Go on over there," Mom said. "Mrs. Witowicz could use some help and some company, too. Having a kid around might take her mind off things and cheer her up."

There was another rap at the screen door. It was Lenny.

"Come on in," Mom called.

Lenny hitched up his leg and made his way

over to the kitchen table, the screen door slapping shut behind him. He sat in Dad's chair.

I grinned. It's a good thing Dad wasn't here to see who was keeping his seat warm.

"Better run upstairs and get dressed, Junior. The gang's all here," Mom said. She set a plate of pancakes in front of Lenny.

When I came back down, Lenny and Bobby were sitting on the back steps playing their harmonicas.

Lenny announced, "I'm going over to Mrs. Stefanski's across the street. Maybe she'll hire me to mow her lawn. Take care of her garden, too, and water her shrubs."

"Can you handle all that?" Bobby asked.

"I can handle it." He could, too. He'd probably work up a good sweat dragging that metal brace around while pushing the mower, but he'd handle it.

"I'd need some help in the garden, though."

"I'll help! That'll be my job!" Bobby said.

"You could help me, Bobby, next door at Mrs. Witowicz's," I said.

"No, thanks! I'm not going anywhere near that haunted shed!"

Chapter Three

Mrs. Witowicz was very happy to hire me. "I like nice yard," she said. "You make nice, just like Benny. Okay?"

Uh-oh.

"I pay. I pay."

I was going to ask how much, but I knew Mom would think that was impolite.

"I pay. Go. Go take lawn mower from shed. Go take."

"That's okay. I'll use my dad's."

"No. No. Use Benny's lawn mower. New. Go take," she said, pushing me forward.

I took a few hesitant steps toward the shed and looked back over my shoulder at her.

Go, she motioned to me.

I stumbled and fell against the shed. Suddenly the door squeaked open. Mrs. Witowicz's fat gray cat leaped out at me.

"Eeeyah!" I screamed. "Yow!"

Mrs. Witowicz laughed. "Just cat. Come on, kitty. Come on."

"I'll be right back," I called. I ran back to my own yard. I opened our basement bulkhead and got Dad's lawn mower from the cellar.

"I'm used to this one," I told Mrs. Witowicz.

"Okay. Okay. Do your way," she said, throwing up her hands.

The morning grew hot. Cutting Mrs. Witowicz's grass took longer than I thought it would. Finally, I was done, and it was time to get paid. I guessed it had been worth it.

"Nice job. Good, good," Mrs. Witowicz said. She smiled and looked around her neat green yard. Then she held out a paper plate covered with waxed paper. "Here. Pay for you, boychik. Stuffed cabbage. I make for you. Here."

I couldn't speak. This was my pay? A plate of stuffed cabbage? Oh, brother!

"Thank you," I said politely.

"You eat. You like," she said, smiling and nodding.

"Thank you," I called over my shoulder as I slouched home.

"Oh, stop your bellyaching!" Mom said. "She paid you, didn't she? Now I won't have to make you lunch."

Bellyaching? I hoped I wouldn't be after I ate the stuffed cabbage.

I wondered how Lenny and Bobby had made out. I joined them across the street at Mrs. Stefanski's.

Mrs. Stefanski was old, too, but not quite as ancient as her friend Mrs. Witowicz. In the shade of the late afternoons, Mrs. Stefanski would go over to sit with Mrs. Witowicz in her yard.

"Why don't you sell your house and move across the street to the second floor of my house? I won't charge much rent," Mrs. Stefanski would say. "Benny's gone now. Sell your house. You won't be so lonely upstairs at my place."

"There's Benny's shed," Mrs. Witowicz would say.

"Forget Benny's shed! It's just a shed with rakes and hoses and shovels. What are you gonna do with a shovel, an old lady like you? What are you gonna dig?"

"I like my own yard."

"Aah! Come fall it's gonna be too cold to sit out in your yard. Come live in my place. We can cook together. We can crochet together. I'll teach you. It's good for the arthritis in your hands."

"My legs hurt. Bad legs. Can't go up and down your stairs."

"Then I'll come upstairs," Mrs. Stefanski would say.

"I have cat. You have dog."

"So they'll learn to get along. Aah!"

✳ ✳ ✳

"So, how'd it go?" I asked Bobby and Lenny.

They were wiping their sweaty foreheads on their arms. "She hired us! Look! We made fifty cents!" Lenny said, holding out his hand.

Wow! Fifty cents!

"Lenny and I are going to keep our money in a shoe box at Lenny's house," Bobby said. "How'd you do?"

"Don't ask!" I said.

But they did. I even told them the part about the cat jumping out at me from the shed. And when they laughed, I laughed a little, too.

Chapter Four

The next day was a scorcher, so Lenny and Bobby and I decided to take some time off from job hunting. We were on our way to the pond to look for frogs.

"Be careful, boys," Mom warned. She always said that, even though she knew the deepest part of the pond came up only to our chests.

We were walking past Chip's Variety Store when we spotted Ricky Rondo. He lived a few houses down the street from me. Ricky had just graduated from high school, but he didn't have a job yet. Maybe it was because of his wisecracking mouth. Maybe it was because of his long, slicked-back, greasy hair. Maybe it was because of his black motorcycle boots with the knife pockets on the sides. He was leaning against the storefront with his two low-life pals.

"Just ignore them," I whispered. "Walk right by." Sometimes Lenny could get cranked up.

"Hey, lookee, lookee!" Ricky called. "The Three Stooges are out for a stroll. Oh, sorry! My mistake! It's Huey, Dewey, and Louie! Quack, quack, quack!"

He started flapping his arms like they were wings. His friends snorted with laughter and slapped him on the back. Then they started quacking, too.

"You birdbrains! Birdbrains!" Lenny answered.

"Ooh, listen to that! Lenny-with-the-leg has something to say to us. Or was that your widdle fwiend Wobbit?"

"Just keep quiet," I said in Lenny's ear.

"Hey, you! Junior Baboonya!" Ricky stepped in front of us, blocking the sidewalk. "Telling secrets about us? Huh? Huh? Tell you what— you and Wobbit and Lenny-with-the-leg go into Chip's and swipe a bottle of soda for me and each of my pals here. Then we'll let you walk on our sidewalk."

Chip's Variety was right across the street

from our school. The store would be full of kids when school let out for the day. Chip always had plenty of what we liked—grape Popsicles, Twinkies, and five-cent bags of potato chips.

Sometimes if we were a penny short, he'd say, "Pay me next time." Later, when we tried to pay up, he'd pretend he didn't know what we were talking about and wouldn't take our money.

"What's the matter? Are you fwaidy cats?" Ricky said.

Uh-oh. I could feel trouble trickle down my back. Lenny never turned down a dare.

"I'll steal you a soda," Lenny said, "but you have to give me something for my trouble. A dime."

Oh, great. There was no holding Lenny back now. And I knew what he was thinking. Another dime toward the raft.

"Now, Lenny. Lenny, Lenny, Lenny. You want I should pay you?"

Ricky turned to his friends and chuckled. "Okay, you got a deal. I'll pay you a quarter, since you asked so pretty."

What had Lenny got us into?

"Get me a Coca-Cola," Ricky ordered.

"Don't be picky," Lenny answered. "You get what you get."

Lenny shoved Bobby into the store. "Keep

Chip busy," he said. "Junior, you come with me."

"What do I say? What do I do?" Bobby blubbered.

"Hey, there!" Chip said from behind the candy counter. "What'll it be today, Bobby?"

"Uh . . . uh . . . my mother wants a deck of playing cards," Bobby said.

Chip raised his eyebrows. "Playing cards? Okay." He reached up behind him for a package.

"No, not the blue ones. They have to be red." Only it sounded like "wed."

I winced. I could hear Ricky outside, snickering and mimicking Bobby.

"My mother wants the red ones. Those are the lucky ones. Do you have any in back?"

"Well, I don't think so, but I'll check." Chip stepped into the back room.

"Quick! Here! Grab this one!" Lenny said, flipping open the cooler. He shoved two cold sodas under his shirt, one under each arm. I didn't know how he could stand it. Just the one under my shirt was bad enough. I headed for the door, Lenny limping behind me.

Chip reappeared behind the counter. "No, no red ones." Then he spotted Lenny and me making a dash for the door. "Hey, you two!"

I made it out just in time.

"Lenny, what you got there?"

Lenny stopped in his tracks.

"You got something under your shirt?" Chip called angrily.

Lenny turned and looked at Chip with big, sad eyes. "No, I didn't take anything, Chip. It's just my new leg brace. It comes up kind of high. It makes it even harder to walk, and it hurts, too. Real bad."

Chip blushed. "Oh, gee, kid. I'm sorry. I didn't know."

Bobby scooted out the door behind us. "Thanks anyway about the cards," he called. "See you."

"I didn't know," Chip continued to apologize.

I couldn't believe what we had just done. My dad would kill me if he knew.

The three of us raced down to the end of the block. Ricky and his friends were right on our heels.

"Okay, kiddies. Hand over the goods."

"Where's the dime?" Lenny asked. "The dime first."

"You mean this dime?" Ricky flipped the coin in the air. "Maybe I changed my mind. Maybe me and my pals are just going to grab those sodas and take off." Flip. Flip. "Maybe—"

Lenny reached up and caught the dime before Ricky could.

"Hey! Hey! You crummy little rat!" Ricky hollered.

Lenny was off and running! Bobby and I were right behind him. It took Ricky a second or two to realize what had happened before he took chase, so we got a head start. With Lenny in the lead, hitching and hopping, we zigged and zagged through yards. Ricky and his friends were catching up. We rounded the corner at Bobby's house and hid in the first-floor hallway. We chuckled as we watched Ricky and his pals run by. When the coast was clear, we moseyed down to Pete's Garage. We'd lost them! We'd lost Ricky and his friends! We leaned against Pete's soda cooler, laughing and congratulating ourselves.

"Whoeee!" Lenny said. "Might as well enjoy!" Pop! He popped the cap off one of the sodas, using the opener on Pete's cooler.

Pop! Pop! I popped my soda, and Bobby popped his. We'd only had time for a couple of swigs when Ricky and his friends skidded to a halt at the corner.

"There they are! The three little goonies!" he said. Ricky stood with his hands on his hips. "Come on!" He motioned for us to hand over the sodas. He stood in front of Lenny, within pushing distance. "I said give 'em here!" he growled.

I'll tell you. I was willing to do just as Ricky said. Ricky had a mean streak. I once saw him push a little kid off a tricycle.

"Let's do what he says," I said, nudging Lenny.

"Yeah, do what he says," Bobby agreed.

Lenny put his thumb over the opening and gave the bottle a good shake. "Okay, okay. Here. It's all yours," he said.

Sploosh! The root beer fizzed and shot out in a stream all over Ricky's white T-shirt.

Ricky jumped back. "Hey, you little—" Then he came at Lenny.

"What's this ruckus out here? What's going on?" a voice boomed behind us.

It was Pete, the owner of the garage. Pete was a big guy. Biceps as big as holiday hams and hands the size of snow shovels. Really big. My dad always took our old car to Pete. Dad said he was an honest mechanic—someone hard to find. One time the Chevy's brakes went right after the radiator was replaced. Pete let Dad "put it on the bill" and pay as he could. But Dad never took advantage, as some people did.

"Pete's a good man," Dad said.

"Too good for his own good," Mom added.

Pete wiped his shovels—I mean hands—on a greasy rag.

"Leave those boys alone!" he yelled at Ricky. "Stop picking on little kids. Remember, there's always somebody bigger than you!" He took a step toward Ricky. "Get lost! Get outta here! Why don't you go get yourself a job, you loafer!"

Ricky and his friends backed away. Ricky shook his fist at us.

"Go on!" Pete said. "Keep going, you bums!"

"Yeah, well, I ain't no bum!" Ricky hollered back, his voice breaking. "I got plans, you know! I got plans!"

The others turned and followed Ricky down the street.

Then Pete turned to us. "You kids didn't swipe those sodas from me, did you?"

"No, Pete. We got them from Chip's," Lenny said.

I don't know. Stealing didn't feel right. A couple of days later, when Mom asked me to go to the store for bread, I went all the way over to Borden's Market instead of to Chip's. It took me two weeks to get up the nerve to walk into Chip's store again.

Bobby had a hard time looking Chip in the eye the rest of the summer.

And one day I saw Lenny take a dime out of his pocket and give it to Chip.

"Here, Chip. I found this on the floor. Customer must've dropped it."

"Well, aren't you some honest kid." Chip beamed. "You keep it."

I think he was still feeling bad for embarrassing Lenny about his leg brace.

"Nah," Lenny said, handing the dime to Chip. "It belongs to the store. It's yours."

✴ ✴ ✴

That afternoon, when the three of us finally got to the pond, Nancy Lewis and her friend Ellen were there. A huge rock sat in the middle of the pond like a little island. Bobby and I would swim out to that rock and pretend we were Robinson Crusoe—that's if the girls weren't around to spoil everything. Darn! The girls had already claimed the rock for themselves. Well, we'd see about that! Bobby and I left Lenny onshore to catch frogs, and we made our way to the rock, too.

"Hi, Junior," Nancy said. "I was going to stop by your house later. I'm having a party next week, and you're invited."

"A party? What for?" I asked.

"Just for fun!"

"You're invited, too, Bobby," Ellen said.

"Will it be a party with cake and games?" Bobby asked.

"Of course!" Nancy said.

"Well, who else is coming?" I asked. I'd never been to a party for no reason before.

"Kids! Kids from school!" Nancy said.

"Is Lenny invited, too?"

"Lenny? No! I'm not inviting that cootie head!" Nancy said.

Bobby looked puzzled. "Lenny doesn't have cooties," he said.

"Well, if Lenny isn't coming, then I'm not either," I said.

"Me neither," Bobby said.

Nancy sighed. "Oh, okay! Lenny can come, too! Two o'clock. Next Tuesday," she said. Then she jumped into the water and swam off.

Ellen smiled. "I know a secret," she sang, sliding into the water.

"What? What secret?" Bobby asked.

Ellen giggled. "Nancy's in love with Junior!" And she swam away, too.

Oh, brother!

✶

Chapter Five

Elvis! Elvis was going to be on television to-night! We all sat down to watch and passed around the bowl of Jiffy Pop popcorn Mom had made.

"Elvis. Hmph. Is he that new singer all the kids have been falling all over?" Dad asked.

"Well, all the girls really like him," Linda said. "But I don't know if you and Mom will."

"I've heard him on the radio," I said. "He sounds pretty good. He plays a guitar."

"Hmph. A guitar," Dad said.

Mom laughed.

"What?" Dad asked.

Mom laughed again. "Joe, you sound old when

you say that." Mom never stopped trying to get Dad to lighten up.

Dad picked up a little pillow from the couch and tossed it at her.

"Old enough to be the father of a high-school graduate," he said. "Junior, how about you and I go outside and throw the ball around for a while before it gets too dark."

I hated to say no to Dad when he was in a good mood and wanted to play ball. Mom heard me sigh.

"It'll just be a few minutes, Joe. Let Junior watch," she said.

And there he was! Elvis Presley!

Girls in the audience were screaming and jumping and crying. I couldn't understand that part. Crying?

"Look how excited they are!" Mom said.

Linda giggled.

"This better be good," Dad said, shaking his head.

Well, Dad got an eyeful right along with the rest of us, right along with the rest of the country. You should have heard the bedlam when Elvis finished his song. More screaming teenage girls were pulling their hair. The television cameras showed a couple of them fainting right in the aisle! Elvis waved, and the girls screamed for more. They stretched their arms out to him as he was quickly whisked off the stage.

Dad jumped up from the couch. He had his hands on his hips and that same look on his face as when he yelled at me about Lenny.

"Did I just see what I think I saw? Is it legal to do that in public? That kind of . . . of . . ."

"Dance?" Mom suggested.

"I'd hardly call that a dance!" Dad said.

I could almost see steam coming out of his ears. Boy, he sure was mad. Why was he getting so angry about Elvis Presley?

"All that . . . that wiggling! Does he have to do all that?"

"Oh, Dad," Linda said.

"Don't you oh-Dad me!" Dad turned to Mom. "And you," he said. "You think this is a good thing for your young son and daughter to watch? Aren't you embarrassed to be sitting here with them right now?"

Mom smiled. "Actually, I think Elvis is kind of cute," she said.

Gee, Mom sure was brave talking to Dad like that.

Dad motioned to me. "Junior, let's go! There's still some daylight left." He got our baseball gloves from the hall.

"Joe, you're taking this too seriously," Mom said. She was always saying that to him. "Joe, relax. It's just a rock 'n' roll act." But Dad was already slamming the screen door on his way outside.

"I think Elvis is a little strange," I said.

"That's because you're a ten-year-old boy," Linda said.

"One thing's for sure—he reminds me of Ricky Rondo, with that slicked-back hair."

Linda poked me. "Oh, Junior! Don't say that! You're spoiling it for me!"

Mom and Linda laughed.

I put on my Red Sox cap—the one Dad bought me at the game we went to in Boston last summer. I joined Dad in the backyard. I hoped he had calmed down. He was inspecting the new brick barbecue pit he'd been working on. His summer project. He wanted to have it ready for our party on the Fourth of July. He saw me coming and threw me the ball.

"Hey, here he is! The president of the Elvis Presley Fan Club!" Dad called.

I pitched it back.

"Not me! That's girlie stuff!" I said.

Catch.

"You liked Elvis," Dad said. "I know you did."

Throw.

"I know *you* did!" I called.

"Yeah, me and my pal Elvis Presley!" Dad said. He laughed again.

I loved it when he joked with me. Why couldn't he be like this all the time? One smile from him could fill me with such a warm, good feeling. Why couldn't he just let go of whatever it was that made him so mad?

"Why does Dad get so wound up sometimes?" I once asked Mom. "It's as if he doesn't like to have fun."

"You've got to remember what it was like for Dad when he was growing up," she said. "His family had it harder than mine. They were very poor. His father lost his life savings during the Depression. Not that Grandpa was rich, but it was all he had. When Dad was your age he had to help earn money for the family to live. He didn't have any time for fun when he was growing up."

I felt bad for my dad when I thought about

him having to quit school to sell newspapers on the street corner.

"When he joined the Army Air Corps during World War II," Mom said, "he saw plenty of bad things happen. What else can I say to help you understand him? He's a good man, Junior. Always trying to make things better, easier for Linda and you and me. Dad is a serious type. Hard-thinking. Hardworking."

Hard. That was him all right. Hard to talk to. Hard to be with. Hard.

Chapter Six

A few days later Mrs. Witowicz asked me to trim her hedges. I wasn't sure if I should. I'd never used the hedge clippers before.

"I pay," she said. "I pay."

I looked at Mom and rolled my eyes. I needed a job that paid money, not food.

Mom gave me a poke. "You go over there and help her out," she whispered. "Do a good deed!"

"Okay, okay. I'll do it," I said.

I came prepared this time. I brought my dad's hedge clippers with me. Now, trimming bushes sounds pretty easy, but it's one of those jobs that just look that way. It took me a lot longer than I thought it would. Old Benny hadn't taken care of the hedges for quite a while, him being sick. I'd been at the job for about an hour when Mrs. Witowicz came out to see how I was doing. I could tell right away by the look on her face that she was sorry she'd ever asked me to do them.

"Oh, short over here. Long over there," she said, frowning. "You cut some more there."

"Okay," I said, wiping my forehead. I sighed and whacked away with the clippers.

"Oh, now long over here. Short over there," she said.

"I guess I'm no good at this," I said with a shrug.

"No, you good boy. You good. Cut lilla bit more. Lilla bit here."

So I cut a little more here and a little more there and . . . well, let's just say Mrs. Witowicz wouldn't be needing her hedges trimmed for a long time.

"Here. For you," Mrs. Witowicz said. She handed me a kielbasa sandwich wrapped in waxed paper. "I pay," she said.

Great. A kielbasa sandwich. I was turning into a real boychik. I wondered how many kielbasa sandwiches the man at the bicycle shop would be willing to trade for a Raleigh.

"Look, Mom," I complained. "She gave me food again instead of money."

"That's her way of treating you well. In her mind that's better pay than money. That's her way. You should be glad she's not complaining about her hedges."

When Dad came home from work that afternoon, he let out a long whistle.

"Whatever happened to Mrs. Witowicz's hedges?" he said.

"For you," I said, handing him the sandwich I had saved.

✳ ✳ ✳

The sound of branches knocking against my window woke me up. Oh, you bet I was terrified. I was scared that whatever was out there was trying to get in. Then, as I became more alert, I realized that we were having a wild windstorm. Then I heard that awful moaning again. I wanted to hide under my blanket, but I decided to be brave and take a look.

The sky was starless. Clouds floated in front of the waning moon. I scanned the dark corners of the yard, searching for anything that might be creeping around. Nothing. Nothing, just nothing. Just wind. After a while my heart stopped racing and I began to feel sleepy again.

Then I heard it! My eyes darted over to Mrs. Witowicz's yard. And I saw it! With one wheezy, woeful moan, old Benny's shed creaked in the wind and fell over on its side. That was the end of it.

The next morning Mrs. Witowicz paid me—potato pancakes—to lug all the old boards and rusty tools to the curb for the trash collector.

✳ ✳ ✳

After supper Dad was lying on the couch, watching the Red Sox on TV win big. Bobby and Lenny came over. We were sitting on the front steps with empty pickle jars, half listening to the ball game, waiting for it to get dark so we could catch lightning bugs. We had to keep it quiet because Dad didn't know Lenny was with us.

Roger pulled up in his red-and-white fins.

"Sh-boom, sh-boom—" He turned the radio down and honked the horn for Linda.

Bobby, Lenny, and I walked over to the car to take a closer look. Maybe one day I'd be driving around in one of those. Who knew? Lenny ran his fingers along the chrome on the door.

"Hey! Get your hands off!" Roger said. He got out of the car to chase us away.

We moseyed back to the steps just as Linda came bouncing out of the house.

"Hi, Roger," she said, smiling. She had on a new pink blouse and an accordion-pleated skirt. Knowing what I knew about Roger being a cheapskate, I didn't understand why she bothered to get all gussied up for him.

Linda reached for the car door handle.

"Whoa there!" Roger said. "Take your shoes off before you get in."

"What?" she asked. "What did you say?"

"I said shoes off."

"Are you serious?"

"New rule. I can see where your shoes have been messing up the floor mat on that side."

"Well, I'm not taking my shoes off," Linda said in a huff. She reached for the handle again.

Roger grabbed her arm. "Hey, I said shoes off!"

I stood up. Bobby stood up. Lenny stood up. I didn't like the way Roger grabbed her arm.

"Leave her alone!" Lenny yelled.

"Yeah, get your hands off her," I joined in.

Was I supposed to run over there and beat him up? Was I supposed to yell for my dad? What was I supposed to do? I didn't know what to do!

Linda knew what to do. She shoved Roger away.

"You listen to me, big shot! Just who do you think you are? I'm not taking off my shoes in anybody's car! Furthermore, I'm sick of how you treat me! From now on, you can buy your own doughnuts! I never want to see you again!"

Linda marched back across the yard.

"Oh, yeah?" Roger hollered.

"Yeah!" Linda answered.

"Fine with me!"

My friends and I cleared out of the way as Linda stomped up the stairs.

She turned and yelled to Roger, "Get lost, loser! Bowling-alley boy!"

"Hey, I'm going to the community college in the fall!" Roger shouted.

Linda shut the screen door behind her as hard as she could. "Yeah, and pigs'll whistle!"

Dad came to the front door. Linda bumped into him as she turned to run up to her room.

"What's going on?" he asked. He opened the screen door and came outside. "What's all this racket out here?" he demanded.

Roger slammed the car door, tires squealing as he took off.

"What happened?" Dad asked, looking at me.

Lenny spoke up. "Don't worry about it. We took care of it," he bragged.

"You!" Dad said, pointing his finger at Lenny. "You! I told you before not to come around here! Stay away from my son! Stay away!"

Lenny picked up his pickle jar. "Okay, okay. I'm going," he said, his voice quivering.

I felt guilty about getting Lenny in trouble. "Dad, it's my fault. I invited him."

But my dad wasn't even listening to me. Bobby picked up his jar, too.

"Bobby, you can stay," Dad said.

But Bobby ran to catch up with Lenny.

"Hey, I said you can stay!" Dad called after him.

"Why are you doing this to me, Dad!" I said, trying not to cry. "Why are you doing this? I'm not going to have a friend left in the world! I wish you weren't my father!"

I let the screen door slam behind me.

"Hey, that's no way to talk to me! You come back here! I said come back here!"

Chapter Seven

I was so relieved when Bobby called me the next morning after Dad left for work. He said to meet him at Lenny's house in ten minutes. He was all excited about something! When I got there I tried to apologize to Lenny about my dad.

"Your dad scares me, too," Bobby said. "But listen—here's why I called you!"

A few days each week Bobby's Uncle Stan went down early in the morning to the farmers' market and loaded up his truck with all sorts of fruits and vegetables. Then he'd peddle them from neighborhood to neighborhood, selling to all the housewives. He often bragged about how much money he made doing this.

"You could help me out! Bring a couple of your pals to help out, too," he'd said to Bobby. "I could use a few extra hands. Sometimes the line at my truck is five, six people long."

Uncle Stan said he'd pay us each fifty cents a day!

"A job like this is just what we've been looking for!" Lenny said, rubbing his hands together. "Take it easy, ride around in the back of a truck all morning, throw a few cucumbers into a bag. My kind of job!"

The next morning Bobby, Lenny, and I showed up right on time. Uncle Stan took one look at us and shook his head.

"Nope, nope, nope." He jabbed his finger in the air at Lenny. "I ain't lettin' no polio kid on my truck. Them housewives take one look at him and nobody's buyin' nothin' from Stanley. People don't want no polio germs on their bananas!"

Lenny's face turned bright red.

Uncle Stanley sounded just like my dad. And was it true? Would his customers be afraid of Lenny?

"Lenny's okay. He doesn't have any more germs," Bobby said. "He goes to school with us and everything."

"Never mind," Lenny said. "It's all right. You

and Junior go." Lenny hung his head and started to walk away.

"Uncle Stan," Bobby said, "tell him he can come. Please."

"Hey, kid," Uncle Stan called. "I don't mean nothin' against you. Unnerstand?"

"It's okay," Lenny called back.

"I'm not going with you either, Bobby," I said.

Lenny saw me chasing after him.

"No, you go with them," he said. "Go. It's okay. I'll ask Mrs. Stefanski if she has something for me to do at her house. Go on." His mouth quivered, and his face began to crumble.

I stood there watching Lenny hitch along the street. I stood there listening to Uncle Stan and Bobby calling me.

"Come on! Time to go!"

"Junior, come on!"

Frozen. My feet were frozen to the sidewalk. This wasn't fair! What was wrong with grown-ups anyway? Didn't they care how they made a kid feel? Bobby yanked the back of my T-shirt.

"He's starting the truck! Let's go!"

I had to decide.

Bobby and I hoisted ourselves up onto the back of Uncle Stan's truck, and we chugged off.

Uncle Stan sure had a lot of customers on his

route, and he was right about needing our help.

"Two pounds of tomatoes, please. Not too red."

"I want three cucumbers. Not the big ones. Too many seeds."

"A dozen ears of corn, please."

"How many in a dozen?" Bobby whispered to me. He always had a hard time with math.

"Any plums today? I'll take three pounds."

"Give me eight peaches."

The peaches were good. Bobby and I sampled a few. It was about eleven o'clock and getting hotter and hotter. Bobby and I were swatting flies off us. Bobby knocked at the window at the back of the cab.

"Uncle Stan," he called, "is it almost time to go home?"

"Go home?" Uncle Stan answered. "We got a coupla more hours on the road!"

A couple of hours?

"I don't know about you, Bobby," I said, "but I've got to have something to drink!"

"Me, too," Bobby said.

Uncle Stan drove into a playground area and parked. He jumped from the truck and plopped himself under a shade tree. He took a swig from his thermos and opened his metal lunch box.

Bobby and I licked our lips.

"Uncle Stan, Junior and I—we didn't bring a lunch. We thought we'd be home by now."

Uncle Stan laughed. "Ha! Peddlin's an all-day job. You kids sure have a lot to learn!" He bit a hunk from his bulging sandwich.

"Uncle Stan, we're real thirsty," Bobby said.

"So what am I supposed to do about it? Two stupid kids come to work without a lunch! Ha!"

"But we've got to have something to drink," Bobby said.

"Hey, I don't got none to spare." He set his thermos closer to his side. "Go get yourselves a drink over there." He pointed to a water fountain.

Bobby and I walked over to it and looked at each other. Just a trickle of water bubbled out from the metal spout. Then I spotted a man with an ice-cream pushcart.

"Look! I'll bet he's got Popsicles. I wish we had Popsicles," I said. I followed Bobby back to his uncle.

"Uncle Stan, can Junior and I have money for a Popsicle? Please? We're hot. I've got a headache."

Uncle Stan finished chewing. "Yeah, yeah. Here." He dug out a handful of change from his pocket and handed Bobby a nickel.

"A nickel? You want Junior and me to share one Popsicle?"

"Oh, you guys!" Uncle Stan groaned. He reached into his pocket for another nickel. "Here. Each of you gets one. Now leave me alone." He took another swig from his thermos. "And I'm takin' a nickel from your pay. Each of you."

Bobby and I hurried over to the ice-cream man. Before I could finish it, half the Popsicle melted in the sweltering heat, painting purple stripes down my arm. The Popsicles were a tease.

Back on the truck, Bobby and I couldn't help ourselves.

"Here," Bobby said, tossing me a nectarine. "Have one of these. They're juicy. Take these, too." He handed me a bunch of grapes.

There was no stopping us now. I had a box of blueberries and a box of strawberries. Then another box of blueberries. A few more streets and a while later, I had another bunch of grapes. By the middle of the afternoon, when we turned onto Grove Street and headed for home, I had also eaten my way through a sack of cherries. Then I heard that rumbling kind of noise only a belly can make. At first I didn't know if it was Bobby's belly or my own. I wasn't feeling very well. Bobby didn't look too perky, either. No mistaking it now. It was my own belly talking. It was getting louder and stronger. Fruit belly.

Just in time, Uncle Stan pulled to a stop in front of my house. I leaped off the truck without even hollering bye. I dashed up the steps and flung open the front door.

"Junior?" Mom said.

I flew past her and up the stairs.

"Junior?" Mom called.

Thank God Linda wasn't in the bathroom, smiling at herself in the mirror as usual. I slammed the door shut.

"Junior, are you all right?"

✺ ✺ ✺

Uncle Stan found out about all the fruit Bobby and I helped ourselves to. He blew his stack. "Just for that, you guys ain't gettin' paid nothin'! And you still owe me for the Popsicles! You're gonna pay!"

Pigs will never whistle.

Chapter Eight

The phone rang as Dad was getting ready to leave for the bowling alley. He belonged to a league with some of his friends from work. It was the head of the local veterans' group calling Dad personally, as he did every year, to ask him to march in the Fourth of July parade.

"A Silver Star hero. We'd be honored to have you march with us, Joe," he said.

"No," my dad answered. "I never wanted to be in the limelight. And I don't want to stir up any dust. I'm sure you understand about that. Just trying to get on with things."

"Joe, why don't you say yes," Mom said. "It might make you feel good. You'd be honoring all of your army buddies, you know. Representing them."

Dad couldn't be convinced.

"Well, at least come with us to the parade this year," Mom said.

"Stop badgering me," Dad said.

I pretended to read my comic book.

Mom sighed. "You have to stop hiding away your feelings. You have to stop hiding away from us. You need to talk to someone about what happened to you in the war. Maybe you should talk to that nice Father Burns down at the church."

"I'm doing all right!" Dad shouted. "Leave me alone!"

Uh-oh. I hoped this wasn't going to be another big fight.

"See! See what I mean?" Mom said. "See how one phone call can set you off? Now we'll all be walking on eggshells around here for the rest of the week. Tiptoeing around your temper."

Dad picked up his bowling bag and started to leave the room. Mom blocked his way and put her hand on his arm.

"Joe, honey, please. You're hurting inside. It's getting worse."

He looked at me and shook his head. "Not now, Carol."

"Yes, now, Joe. That little boy pretending to read his comic book—well, you can bet he's taking this all in. And he needs to know that war heroes aren't really tough guys at all. He needs to know that fathers are human beings who have soft, feeling hearts."

"Carol . . . I can't. Just let things be, all right?"

"Oh, Joe," Mom said. She put her arms around his stiff ones and hugged him gently.

"I have to go. I'll be late for bowling," he said, pushing her away.

Mom was right. Dad needed to talk about whatever it was that was bothering him. We could help him get over it.

"Mom, was it real bad for Dad in the war?" I asked.

"Yes, it was bad. I only know a little about what happened. Dad won't even talk to me. I don't know. Maybe he needs a doctor."

Mom was scaring me. "Is he sick?" I asked.

"See! Now there I go getting you all upset." She gave a little laugh and hugged me. "Dad will be all right. Everything will work out."

But I could see the worry in her eyes.

✸

Chapter Nine

Mom was in our backyard hanging laundry out when Nancy's mother stopped by to chat.

"Junior, you didn't tell me Nancy Lewis invited you to a party," Mom said later.

"I was going to tell you tomorrow," I said.

"But the party's tomorrow."

"I know."

"Boys . . ." Mom said, shaking her head. "Well, I think it's really nice of the Lewis family to invite Lenny, too. Poor kid. He's been treated like such an outcast in this town. I'm glad we still have some reasonable people around."

The next day Mom made me take a bath, and it was only a Tuesday. She even combed Brylcreem through my hair and made a neat side part.

"Wear your church shirt and your bow tie," she ordered.

"Mom! Not the bow tie!"

"Yes, you're wearing it. Put it on. You boys run loose all summer looking like hooligans. It'll do you good to clean up. Even on a Tuesday."

I made faces at myself in the mirror as I clipped on the bow tie.

Mom caught me at it. "Stop that! And don't forget your manners while you're at the party." She put a box of candy in my hands. "Give this to Nancy."

"What? A present? It's not her birthday!"

"This is a hostess gift. Nancy and her mother are going to a lot of trouble for this party. Be nice."

"But, Mom . . ."

"Go! Go!" she said, pushing me out the door. "And be nice!"

Bobby and Lenny were waiting for me at the corner, and we walked to Nancy's together.

"Why did she have to go and have a party anyway?" I said.

"Yeah, we could be down at the pond right now looking for turtles or toads," Bobby said.

Sometimes we'd catch a bunch of toads and make a Toad Town. We'd get a big cardboard box from the variety store, fill it with dirt, and make houses out of Jell-O boxes. We'd smooth little roads and drive our Matchbox cars around. Toad Town gave us an excuse to play with our little cars again. We'd plop the toads into our box town and watch them settle into their new home.

Once we made Salamander City, but it didn't work out. Overnight the salamanders got cold, or they dried out or something, and the next morning they were all dead. We had better luck with toads. Toads were tough.

"I don't know. The party might be fun," Lenny said.

"I'd rather be looking for turtles or toads," I said, fingering my shirt collar. Lenny hadn't worn his bow tie, and Bobby didn't own one.

I was thinking about taking the tie off as we stood on Nancy's fancy porch, ringing her doorbell. Too late. Mrs. Lewis opened the door.

"Well, boys, don't you look handsome! My, my! Come right in! Such little men!" she said.

She led us through the coolness of her living room. My eyes darted everywhere. I glimpsed the piano Nancy was always bragging about. I stole a peek at the dark wood china closet in the dining room.

"Nancy's having the party downstairs in our new recreation room—our rec room. We put a new hi-fi down there, and there's a little refrigerator for cold sodas. Wait till you see! Come on!"

We followed her down the stairs into the finished basement room.

"Here are your guests, Nancy," Mrs. Lewis said. "I'll bring down the cake later."

"Cake?" asked Bobby. "Okay!"

"I ordered it special from the bakery," Mrs. Lewis said.

"Mmm . . . I love cake!"

Mrs. Lewis smiled. "Well, you all enjoy yourselves. I'll be right upstairs."

"I handed Nancy the box of chocolates.

"A hostess gift," I said. I wanted to make sure she understood it wasn't a real present.

"Thank you, Junior," Nancy said. She smiled and twirled in her pink party dress as she set the box down.

Ellen giggled. She and Ellen had sure gotten all fancied up.

"When are the other kids going to be here?" I asked.

"The others couldn't make it," Nancy said.

She didn't seem very sad or disappointed. Ellen giggled again. Nancy put a record on the hi-fi.

"Let's dance!" Nancy said. "I love the bunny hop!"

Da-da, da-da, da-da—hop, hop, hop.

"Come on!" Nancy called. "Get behind me!"

Hop, hop, hop.

I looked over at Bobby, and we both rolled our eyes.

"How about a cold soda?" Bobby asked.

"First the dancing, then the soda," Nancy said.

"How come?" Bobby asked.

"Because I said so."

Hop, hop, hop.

Bobby and I joined Lenny on the couch. He'd found some Little Lulu comics under the cushion, and Bobby and I pulled out a couple more.

"Listen, you can't read comics! This is a party!" Nancy whipped the books out of our hands. "Let's do the hokey-pokey! Come on, Junior," Nancy said, pulling me to my feet.

Ellen dragged Bobby up, too.

Lenny laughed at us from the couch. I stood still, glaring at him. I wasn't going to hokey—or pokey. Bobby put his left hand in and his left hand out. Then he joined Lenny and me back on the couch.

Mrs. Lewis appeared at the bottom of the stairs. "How are things going?" she asked. "Everyone having a good time?"

Nancy stomped her foot and pouted. "The boys won't dance, Mommy! Make them dance!" she whined.

"Now, Nancy. If the boys don't want to dance, they don't have to."

"But they're spoiling my party," Nancy said.

"Why don't you play a game," Mrs. Lewis said. "Everyone likes games. Now, have fun."

"Is it time for the cake?" Bobby asked.

Mrs. Lewis smiled. "Pretty soon." Then she went upstairs again.

"Let's play drop the clothespins in the bottle," Ellen suggested.

Ellen and Nancy got a handful of clothespins from the laundry room, and Nancy hunted for a milk bottle.

"I could only find this," she said, holding up an empty soda bottle.

"Oh, we can't use that," Ellen said. "The clothespins won't fit."

"That's okay," Nancy said, grinning. "I know

another game." She sat on the floor and motioned for the rest of us to join her. "Well, come on. Sit down."

"What game is this?" I asked.

"You'll see. Everyone, sit in a circle. Everyone!"

"I don't want to play," Bobby said.

"If you don't play, you're not getting any cake—and it's chocolate!" Nancy said.

Bobby hesitated. "Oh, okay."

Lenny joined us, stretching his leg out on the floor. He sat next to Nancy. "I know this game." He smiled.

"Ha! How do you know this game?" she asked.

"Oh, I heard about it. It's called spin the bottle."

Nancy frowned at Lenny. Smiling at me, she said, "This game is called spin the bottle. I spin the bottle. If it points to you, you win!"

"What do you win?" Bobby asked.

"You'll see. I go first, because it's my party."

Nancy spun the bottle around. When it stopped, it was pointing at Lenny.

Lenny grinned. "I win," he said.

"No, you don't!" Nancy said. "I was practicing. The next one counts."

She spun the bottle again, and again it stopped and pointed at Lenny.

"Two out of three!" Nancy said. "That's the rule."

She spun. The bottle pointed at Lenny—again. Before Nancy could say another word, Lenny leaned right over and planted a big kiss on her lips.

Eew! Yuck! Yuck! I thought, how could he do that?

"Eew! Yuck!" Nancy shrieked, jumping to her feet. She scrubbed her lips.

"You creep! You cootie head! I hate you!" she screamed.

Mrs. Lewis stood at the foot of the stairs, holding a beautiful decorated cake.

"Nancy, what's the matter? What is it, sweetheart? What's wrong?" she asked.

Nancy sobbed into her mother's skirt.

"Tell them to go home, Mommy! Tell them to go home!"

Lenny and I clambered past them up the stairs through the living room and out the door. As soon as we got outside, I yanked off the bow tie and unbuttoned my collar. Lenny and I laughed all the way to the corner. Bobby was running right behind us. Finally, he caught up.

"We didn't even get cake!" he complained.

Chapter Ten

"Let's change and meet down at the pond," I said.

"I've got a better idea!" Lenny said. "I went down to Chip's yesterday, and wait till you see what I got with my allowance!"

"What?" Bobby and I both asked.

"A huge bag of plastic army men! A whole platoon! A whole regiment!"

"Wow!" I said. My dad never let me buy any kind of army toys. "We can set them up in my backyard."

"No, you and Bobby better come to my house," Lenny said.

I blushed. I still felt awful about how my dad

had yelled at Lenny. "My mom said you can come over anytime, Lenny. And my dad's at work."

Bobby didn't have much of a yard. He lived at the end of the street near Pete's Garage, right across from the Mansfield-Davis Mill. His three-decker tenement was a run-down place. Peeling paint and litter all around.

Bobby shifted from one foot to the other. "Will you two make up your mind!"

I wanted to make it up to Bobby and Lenny for the way my father had acted. "My mom bought a half gallon of ice cream. The kind with three flavors—vanilla, chocolate, and straw-berry. We can have ice-cream cones!"

"Mmm," Bobby said. "Let's play at his house, Lenny."

"I don't know. My parents said not to," Lenny said. But I could tell he was considering it.

"Come on, Lenny! My mom wants you to come over."

"Oh, okay. But not for long. Just for a half hour or so. I can't be there when your dad comes home."

Bobby started asking about the ice-cream cones as soon as he got to my house, so Mom gave us each a double scoop right away. After that she hunted around for some old washcloths we could use to make tents in the backyard for the soldiers. We dug a shallow trench and made foxholes for the green plastic men. After a while we had a whole camp set up. Some of the figures even had little parachutes attached with string, and we stood on the metal lawn chairs, dropping the men onto targets.

"Junior, your father will be home soon," Mom called. "You boys need to pack up the toys and put this yard back in order."

"Okay," I answered. I lobbed a stone at one of Lenny's men and knocked it over.

"Oh, yeah!" Lenny said. Then he threw a couple of stones at my men.

"Vadoom . . . eeyou!" Bobby's grenades landed with sound effects.

"Baboom . . . baboom!"

We all got into it.

"Eeyou . . . voom!"

We were making such a racket in the backyard that we didn't hear my father's car pull into the driveway. Suddenly I heard the car door slam.

"Hurry up! My dad's home!" I said.

The three of us scrambled to pick up the army men.

I could hear my mother trying to keep my father away from the back door. "Supper is almost ready, Joe. Why don't you come sit with me in the living room and have a nice cold soda?"

Too late. My dad poked his head out the back door.

"Hi, Junior. What you got there?" he asked.

Before I could answer, he spotted Lenny.

"It's you again!" he said, marching toward Lenny. "What are you doing here? And what's this junk? He kicked at one of the army men. "You think the army is play? You think war is fun and games?"

He bent down and picked up one of the soldiers. He threw it at Lenny. "Get this stuff out of here! All of it!" He picked up another soldier and flung that one at Lenny, too.

"Stop!" Lenny said. "That hurts!"

"I'll show you what hurts, you smart mouth!" Dad threw another plastic soldier at Lenny. Then another. And another.

"Please! Stop!" Lenny said, shielding his face with his arms.

"Joe, leave him alone," Mom pleaded.

"Pick it up! Pick it up!" Dad screamed.

Bobby, Lenny, and I couldn't pick up the men fast enough. We were so scared we kept dropping the ones we had in our hands.

"I'll help you!" Dad said. "Here! Here!" And he kept throwing them at Lenny.

"Dad, don't! Leave Lenny alone!" I yelled.

Mom pulled on Dad's arm. "Joe, Joe! Look at yourself! What are you doing?"

"You get this yard cleaned up, Lenny! And the next time you look down at your leg—your sick leg—you just remember that those were real men in the army. Real men who lost real legs. And you just be glad you still have your own!"

Lenny scrambled to his feet. He and Bobby hurried out of the yard. They were both crying. Lenny, the bravest kid in the whole neighborhood—Lenny, who stood up to punks like Ricky Rondo! Dad was making Lenny cry so hard he could hardly catch his breath.

"I hate you! I hate you!" I sobbed, beating my father with my fists.

Mom pulled me away, and I ran into the house and up to my room. I lay on my bed crying. Why did Dad have to go and do that? I'll never forget what he did, I thought. Never! I'll hate him for the rest of my life!

✳ ✳ ✳

Sometime later Mom came upstairs and sat on my bed.

"Oh, God! I've got such a headache!" she said. "It took a while to calm your father down."

She saw my puffy eyes and my red, runny nose. "Looks like I'm going to have to work on you, too," she said, handing me some tissues.

I sat up, and she put her arms around me.

"Poor Junior," she said. "I know you don't understand any of this. Maybe someday you will."

"I hate him! I wish he were dead!" There. I'd said it.

"Stop talking like that!" she ordered. "That's an awful thing to say. You know you love your dad. Remember all the good times you have with him when you're playing ball together. Your father's a good man. He takes care of his family. He loves you."

"Well, how does he show it? By embarrassing me? By picking on my friends?"

"When your father was in the war, he saw a lot of people die. He's afraid you'll get polio from

Lenny. He's afraid you'll die. He couldn't take that. He'd die too if that ever happened to you. He loves you that much."

"That isn't true! He's mean! He's always yelling at me about something! Look how mean he was to Lenny!"

"Dad's not the only person who's afraid of polio. A lot of people are. It's a terrible disease. Remember, Lenny almost died."

"Why can't Dad be like you? Why can't he just calm down?"

"He's working on it," Mom said. "He really is." She sat with me for a few more minutes. "Come on now. I have supper for you in the kitchen."

"I don't want to eat, Mom."

"Yes. You'll feel better. Come on down."

After I ate, Mom called me over to the window. Dad was working on his brick barbecue pit. "I want you to go out and apologize to him for punching him and yelling at him."

"I can't. Don't make me," I pleaded.

"Yes, you have to. He's your father, and you shouldn't have been disrespectful."

"But, Mom, what about what he did?"

"Just go. Make peace." And she pushed me out the door.

I stood next to him for a while, not saying anything. I turned and saw Mom standing at the window. I knew I had to get this over with.

"Dad . . . I'm sorry I hit you and said mean things."

My dad didn't answer. He kept mixing that cement. Mixing and mixing. He didn't even look at me.

"Dad, do you need any help?" I asked.

Still no answer.

"Dad?"

"No. I don't need any help. I just want to be alone. Thanks."

Chapter Eleven

Mom took me to the dentist the next day for my checkup. Then she dragged me along on errands, too. We took the bus downtown to pay some bills, and she bought herself some new shoes and some nail polish for Linda. On the way home we stopped at the market for lunch meat for Dad and Linda, and she let me get a box of Cracker Jacks. It's a good thing she kept me busy all day, because neither Bobby nor Lenny would be calling me up or coming to my house today, or for a while—or probably ever again.

But we did have some unexpected company that night—Lenny's father.

Mom was washing dishes, and Dad and I were

watching President Eisenhower on TV. The doorbell rang for the second time.

"Somebody get that! I'm busy in here!" Mom called from the kitchen.

"Junior," Dad said, motioning for me to answer the door.

I was surprised to see Lenny's father standing on our front steps. This was the first time he'd ever come to our house. He didn't look too friendly.

"Dad!" I called. "Someone to see you!"

"Well, who—Tom!" Dad said, appearing behind me.

"I'm here about what happened yesterday," he said from the other side of the screen door.

"Hi, Tom!" Mom said, joining us in the doorway. "Come on in."

"No, we can talk here," Dad said.

"Joe, for heaven's sake!" Mom said.

"It's all right. I can say what I have to right here," Lenny's father answered. "Joe, my son came home hysterical yesterday afternoon. You threw things at him. You humiliated him."

"I don't want him around here. I've told him that—many times," Dad said.

"Yeah, but you're going too far, Joe. Believe

me, when I found out what happened yesterday, I wanted to come here and give you more than just a piece of my mind."

"Hmph," Dad said.

"I took time to cool off, but I've still got plenty to say to you!"

"Listen, your kid has a sassy mouth, and I don't want him influencing Junior."

"Well, Lenny's no angel. I'm the first one to admit that. I guess I'm not as strict a dad as you are. But, you know, the war's over, Joe. I'm not a decorated hero like you, but I did my part. Now it's time for us all to be good neighbors and enjoy the good life we fought so hard for."

Dad threw open the door, and Lenny's father stepped back onto the lawn.

"Joe . . ." Mom warned.

"I brought these over for you," Lenny's dad said. He held out some papers. Dad took them and glanced at them.

"What's this?"

"They're articles about polio. Read them. You might learn something. And there's a copy of a letter from the school department saying Lenny is allowed to attend public school. If the town of Mansfield accepts Lenny, why can't you?"

Dad threw the papers out into the yard. "You can keep this trash," he said. "Don't you understand? I don't want Lenny here! I don't care what your papers say. He's got that sickness, and he's a danger!"

Lenny's father bent down to gather up the documents. "You know, Joe, you're the danger! If you only knew the physical and emotional pain Lenny has to put up with because of his 'sickness.' I've never seen such courage! Yes, he has a sickness through no fault of his own. But you— you have a sickness in your heart. And you do have the power to do something about it."

Dad slammed the door.

"Don't!" he warned Mom. "Don't you start with me, too! Just stay out of my way!" And he went out into the backyard.

"It's best to let him be," Mom said. "Puttering helps him think."

Chapter Twelve

Ted Williams. I was reading about him in the newspaper when Linda poked her head into my room.

"Hey, little brother!"

She knew I hated it when she called me that.

"Don't you get a headache lying around up here in this hot room all the time?" she asked.

It had been days now since I'd seen Lenny or Bobby. I'd probably seen the last of them for the rest of my life.

Linda started looking through the stack of sports magazines I'd dug out from under my bed. I grabbed them away from her.

"Leave my stuff alone, will you!" I said.

"Hey, I'm trying to be nice. I feel bad for you, with no one to pal around with. It's crummy what happened with Dad and Lenny."

"Well, when I'm a father, I'm never going to be like Dad."

Linda sat at the end of my bed. I could tell she wasn't going away anytime soon. The funny thing was I didn't mind all that much. I guess I was that lonesome.

"What can I say? Dad is Dad." Linda shrugged. "He's got a temper, and he's hard to please. But he's a good person."

"Ha! How can you say that? Even after he's been hanging up on Roger? Roger's been calling you. Did you know that?"

Linda laughed. "Yes, I know. The way Dad always hurries to answer the phone lately! How many wrong numbers can there be? Once I even heard him say I wasn't home!"

"You don't care? Doesn't that make you mad?" I asked.

"Actually, no. I meant what I told Roger. I never want to go out with him again. Dad was right. Roger's rude, and he has no ambition. And I like how Dad scares Roger away. It makes me feel good when my father sticks up for me."

"Like Lenny's father sticks up for him?"

"Yes, I guess it's the same thing. You know, it's more than what it seems," Linda said. "Not only is Dad worried about you getting polio but those army toys set him off, too."

"Why? Why is me playing with little plastic army men such a big deal to him? Why does everything have to be such a big deal?"

Linda sat cross-legged on my bed and sighed. "If only you knew what it was like when Dad came home from the war. I was about six years old. And you were just a twinkle in his eye, as they say."

I blushed. "Yeah, whatever that means," I said. I thought I knew.

"Anyway, I was only six, and I didn't even know him except from pictures Mom had shown me and stories she'd told me about him. I was an infant when he went into the army, you know. Well, there he was—tall, big guy. Loud, deep voice. Scared the knee socks off me. He didn't know what to say to me or how to act with me, either. I was a baby when he left, and here I was a kid already."

"So was he mean to you?" I asked.

"No. Not mean. Impatient sometimes. It just

took a while for us to get used to each other. I could tell he and Mom had missed each other, though."

"Ick. Don't tell me any of that icky, girlie stuff."

"Okay, I won't!" she said, hitting me with the newspaper. "But now when I think about those times I realize how sweet and sensitive he was with Mom."

"Dad? Sweet and sensitive?" Was she talking about my father? The monster who yelled at my friends and threw and kicked toys at a kid with a leg brace?

"Yes. Even the toughest guy has a heart that beats. Every one of us has a place inside that aches and pinches. Dad included. And I think Dad has a real big hurt. One that throbs."

"Huh! Dad?" Mom kept saying things like that, too. What? What was this all about?

"Well, I guess I can't blame you for not under-standing any of this. I didn't when Dad first came home. Believe me."

Linda just sat there quietly.

"What happened? Tell me!" I had to know Dad's big secret.

"Oh, Junior, it was scary. Dad waking up screaming. Screaming about a fire and shouting out names. Names of guys he had been in the war with. I'd jump out of my own bed and run to Mom and Dad's room. I'd stand at the door afraid to go in, afraid to go back to my own room. 'It's all right, Linda,' Mom would say. 'It's all right. Dad had a nightmare. Just a bad dream.'

"Dad would be sitting up in bed, shaking and sobbing. My big, strong father who'd hoist me up on top of his shoulders when we went to the ice-cream store. My big, strong father who'd make bad dogs on the street turn and run away. My dad screaming out in the night about dead soldiers."

I sat quietly with my chin in my hands. "I'm sure glad he doesn't do that anymore. That would scare me, too."

"Well, I don't think bad memories—the kind Dad has—ever go away. Time helps you get over some things, but I think Dad still has most of those army days on his mind."

"But all that happened years ago," I said. "Those army days are over."

"I guess some people can move on and some can't."

"So what's going to happen with Dad if he

can't get on with things?" Mom was right, I thought. He should talk about the war instead of trying to hide it from us.

Linda patted my shoulder. "We'll just have to keep trying to help him. I know it's hard for you, the way Dad's carrying on about Lenny. You're trying to sort things out. Trying to put things together. I guess I've gotten used to it."

The phone rang downstairs. We heard Dad answer it. "Hello? Linda's not home! And stop calling here!"

Linda and I laughed.

"Roger's been driving by, you know," I confessed. "He came by again the other day."

"Well, if he stops and asks you about me—"

"I'll tell him you went out on a date with someone else!"

Linda laughed again. "Thanks, little brother."

Chapter Thirteen

Mom put me to work in the kitchen.

"You're making a cake today. Betty Crocker," she said to me. She handed me a box of one of those new cake mixes.

"But, Mom, I don't know anything about baking cakes!"

"Well, you're going to learn, aren't you! Don't worry, I'll help you."

"I don't know about this," I said, shaking my head.

She smiled and winked at me. "It's for Lenny and his family. We're going to make this cake and take it over to them. A peace offering. This ugly business has gone on long enough."

We were going to Lenny's house? What would Dad say if he knew? Would Lenny's mother even let us in? Would they eat our cake? They might think we were trying to poison them. Would Lenny even talk to me?

After we baked and frosted the cake, Mom and I took a walk over to Lenny's house. Lenny and Bobby were in the yard looking over their baseball cards.

Lenny looked up in surprise. "Junior! Mrs. Webster!"

"Hi!" Bobby said.

"Hello, boys," Mom answered.

Lenny's mother came to the door. "Carol! I'm so glad you're here! Come on in. I've been so upset."

Mom carried the cake inside. I was left standing there watching Bobby and Lenny. They were both ignoring me. I didn't know whether I should go into the house with my mom or just go on back home.

"I'm sorry about how my father acted," I said.

"Yeah!" Lenny finally answered. "He's a lunatic!"

Suddenly my embarrassment changed to anger.

"He is not!" I said. "He's a good guy. You don't really know him like I do."

"Well, my father says he's a lunatic! And I'm never going to your house again! Never!"

"Me either!" Bobby said.

"You guys are jerks!" I said. How could I explain about my dad? "Plain old jerks!" I turned and headed out of the yard.

"Oh, yeah?" Lenny called.

"Yeah!"

Then something hit me in the leg. I picked it up. It was a baseball card with a picture of my favorite Red Sox player, Ted Williams.

Lenny and Bobby walked over to me.

"You can have it," Lenny said.

"Thanks," I said, brushing my eyes with the back of my hand. I dug into my pocket and took out my Cracker Jack prize—a plastic magnifying glass.

"You can have it if you want it," I said, handing it to Lenny.

"Sure," he said. He held it up to his eye and peered at Bobby and me. We all laughed.

"I only have about ten of these," he said.

And we laughed again.

Chapter Fourteen

I admit, I was just about to give up the idea of having a bike this summer. I'd managed to save most of my allowance, but that didn't even come close to what a bike cost. My oatmeal bank was almost empty. And I had to dip into it for personal expenses. Lenny, Bobby, and I decided to use some of our money to see the 3-D movie *The Lizard That Ate Lonsdale*, which was playing in Valley Falls. The newspaper was full of ads for a week before the movie came out. Bobby, Lenny, and I were all hopped-up about it.

"Wow! I have to see this!" Bobby said.

"Need to see it!" Lenny agreed.

"We'll have to take the bus to Valley Falls," I said. I was so glad we were friends again.

"My mother will let me," Lenny said. "How about yours, Bobby?"

"She'll let me. Junior?"

"I guess so. Sure."

I did some quick math. Twenty-five cents for the bus both ways, fifty cents for the movie, twenty-five cents for soda and popcorn—a dollar and twenty-five cents. Most of what I had saved. Well, did I want a bike or did I want to see what was probably the best movie to be made in my lifetime? Like I said, sad as it made me feel, the picture of me pedaling down Grove Street this summer was fading anyway.

Friday afternoon we met at Bobby's house. The bus stopped right there to let off the second-shift workers at the Mansfield-Davis Mill. Then it would return to Valley Falls, bringing us to the Starlite Theater.

The bus slowed to a stop. *Pchooo.* The doors opened, and Bobby, Lenny, and I were eager to jump on.

"Whoa! Let these people off first," the driver said.

I thought the bus would never empty.

"All right! Let's go!" the driver said, motioning to us.

I was the first one on. I loved plunking my

money into the slot and watching the coin zigzag its way down the chute. I stood there watching the quarter do its work.

"Come on, come on, come on!" the driver scolded. "Sit down, will ya!"

Bobby climbed on behind me, and then Lenny hitched his way up the steps and down the aisle. We headed for the back of the bus. The best place to sit. More bounce.

"My mother almost didn't let me come, you know," Bobby confessed. "She said if I had nightmares she didn't want me waking her up."

"For heaven's sake! You're not exactly a baby!" Lenny said.

"I know."

"When Linda and her friend Rita saw *The Lizard That Ate Lonsdale*, Linda screamed so much her tonsils hurt," I said.

"Girls! What do you expect? No movie ever made me scream—not even *The Creature from the Black Lagoon*," Lenny said.

"Do you think there could be such a thing as a fifty-foot lizard living in an underground canal? Right below our street? Right under our own houses?" Bobby asked.

"It's just a movie," I said.

"Yeah, but just imagine!" Lenny said. "Scabby, stubby legs creeping through sewer pipes coated with a hundred years of slime. That long lizard tongue flicking, flicking. Glazed, lidless popeyes, searching. Razor-sharp claws grabbing, scratching frantically for a way out."

Bobby squirmed in his seat.

"First of all, how could a lizard that huge live in a narrow sewer pipe? That could never happen," I said.

"Yeah!" Bobby agreed.

"Listen, you guys, lizards can squeeze down to nothing, just like mice. Lizards are related to snakes, you know. It's the snake in them," Lenny argued. "On *You Asked for It* on TV a few weeks ago, there was a lady who found snakes crawling right out of her toilet."

"Eew!" Bobby said.

"You're so full of baloney!" I said to Lenny.

He laughed.

When we finally got to the Starlite Theater, there was a line a block long. Kids our age. Some with a mother or a father. Some alone, like us. Teenagers, too.

At last the ticket window opened and the line started to move. I was hoping the tickets wouldn't be sold out by the time we got to the window. We just made it!

About five kids after us, an usher came out and made the announcement: "The two o'clock movie is sold out. Next showtime is at four-thirty. Selling tickets now for four-thirty."

"Ohhh . . ." Everyone behind us started groaning and complaining.

Lenny, Bobby, and I smiled and poked at each other. Another usher handed each of us a pair of 3-D glasses.

Lenny put his on and stuck his arms straight out, like Frankenstein's monster. "Follow me to Zombie Land," he said.

I'll tell you, with his leg brace he could do a really good monster impression.

Bobby whispered in my ear, "Do you think a lizard could really live in a sewer pipe?"

"It's just a movie, Bobby," I told him.

Lenny went ahead to save us some seats while Bobby and I got the popcorn and sodas. Just as the movie was starting, we made our way down the aisle of the darkened theater. The good seats up close had already been taken, but Lenny had found us some way back in the fifth row. We let him have the aisle seat because of his leg.

It was weird with everyone sitting there wearing those spooky-looking cardboard glasses. We all looked like lizards ourselves. To tell you the truth, though, I was kind of disappointed. The movie wasn't nearly as scary as all the ads said it would be. My tonsils were doing just fine. The lizard was really silly-looking, and I'd seen better Halloween costumes on first-graders. I even heard Lenny laughing. And to think I had spent my bike money on this! At least we got to keep the 3-D glasses.

Bobby was another story, though. I saw him cover his eyes a few times, and once when I heard the girls next to us scream I thought I heard Bobby scream, too. I think his mother knew what she was talking about—Bobby and his nightmares. When we got up to leave, I saw a big wet spot on Bobby's pants. So did Lenny.

"Hey, what happened to you?" Lenny said, laughing.

"I—I spilled my soda!" Bobby answered, turning bright red.

"Yeah, you sure you didn't pee your pants?"

"No! I spilled my soda, okay!" Bobby said.

I don't know, but just to be certain I wasn't ever going to sit in Row E, Seat 2, at the Starlite Theater.

---------------------------- ✳ ----------------------------

Chapter Fifteen

"You know, we really haven't done any serious fishing this summer," Lenny said.

"What are you talking about? We've been to the pond lots of times," I said.

"No, I mean serious fishing. Let's go down to the river on the other side of the mill."

"Uh-uh. My mother will kill me if I go there. She doesn't want me anywhere near that river. She doesn't want me near the train tracks, either."

"Let's go!" Bobby said. "We'll be careful."

"We'll meet at the corner in ten minutes with our gear," Lenny said. He took off toward home.

"Hey!" I called. "I said I can't go there!"

"Aw, come on, Junior!" Bobby said. He started walking toward his house. "Come on!"

I sighed. I guess if we were careful it would be okay. I ran back home to get my pole and my tackle box.

My mother was on the phone in the hall, making Fourth of July plans. She looked out the window and smiled and waved to me as I passed through the yard. Mrs. Stefanski's dog, Buster, crossed the street and followed me to Bobby's house.

"Go home, Buster!" Lenny yelled. "We don't need that dog chasing after our bobbers in the water. Go home!"

Buster stood there whining and looking at us with his sad dog eyes.

"Go home, Buster," I told him.

After we turned the corner, I looked over my shoulder. Sure enough, there was Buster trotting right behind us. I smiled. It was hard not to like that funny old dog. I poked Bobby.

"Look."

"Oh, great," he said.

We were just about to cross the train tracks when Buster ran ahead of us. He was sniffing the ground, going crazy.

"Good. Maybe he'll chase something and leave us alone," Lenny said.

No sooner had he said that than Buster dashed over to the opening of the culvert that ran under the road to the other side of the street.

"I wonder what he's after," I said.

Buster stood at the end of the culvert, barking up a storm.

"Let's go see," I said.

Buster pounced in front of the culvert and growled.

"What is it, boy?" Lenny asked. "What's in there?"

We peered in, trying to see what that dog was so fired up about. The culvert was fairly high at our end, high enough for a kid my size to walk in without having to stoop too much. It narrowed toward the other end, though, so that you'd have to crawl. My mother said the culvert was a danger, and the least the town should do was put a grate over it so kids wouldn't be tempted to explore. But there it was, wide open. The summer had been so dry that there wasn't even a trickle of water flowing through.

Buster stuck his head in. After his eyes adjusted to the darkness, there was no stopping him.

"Buster!" I yelled. "Come back here! Come on, boy!"

All we needed was for something to happen to Mrs. Stefanski's dog. Then we'd all be in trouble.

"Here, Buster!" Lenny called.

We couldn't see him anymore, but we could hear his excited barking echoing in the pipe.

"He's found something in there," Lenny said.

"What do you think it is? A cat? A mouse?" Bobby asked.

Then Buster started howling and yelping. The echo was ear-piercing. The three of us called to him again.

"He must be stuck at the narrow end and doesn't know how to turn around to get back out," Lenny said.

Someone was going to have to go in there to help him.

"Go get him, Junior," Bobby said.

"Me? Why me?"

"He likes you the best. He'll do what you say. Go get him."

"Aw, gee! Buster, you better not be getting me

into trouble," I said. I took off my baseball cap and tucked it into my back pocket. I ducked my head and started in, trying not to touch the slimy sides. Scenes from *The Lizard That Ate Lonsdale* flashed in front of me.

"Come here, boy. Come here," I coaxed.

At first I could barely make him out in the dark. Just as we'd thought—he'd gone after a cat. I could see it now up a ways. I got down on my hands and knees and crawled toward the dog.

"Here you are, boy. Leave the kitty alone. All you have to do is back up a little and turn around."

I reached out and took hold of his collar. He was nervous and tried to pull away. Nothing like wrestling with a strong dog in a dark, narrow culvert.

"Aw, Buster. Come on."

Then I felt the spray—or did I smell it first?

"Oh, geez! Get out of here, Buster! Get out!" I shoved his big behind out of there as fast as I could.

"Skunk! There's a skunk in here!" I yelled. The skunk continued to spray my arms and legs. It got me good.

Buster made it to the end of the culvert, and I came out tripping over him.

Bobby and Lenny were bent over laughing, slapping their legs.

"You smell awful!" Bobby said.

"This isn't funny!" I answered. I held my shirt out, away from my body.

"You won't be wearing that shirt anymore," Lenny said. He and Bobby were laughing so much they sounded like a couple of squealing pigs.

"Just knock it off!" I said. I felt for my hat. Oh, no. Not that, too. It wasn't as wet as my shirt, but it was wet enough.

Buster was jumping around us in circles. Everyone was sure having a good time except me.

"Thanks, Buster. That's what I get for trying to help you out."

Now, how was I going to explain this to my mother? Bobby and Lenny followed me back to Grove Street, keeping their distance. Even Buster wouldn't walk with me.

"Mom, Mom," I called through the back screen door. I knew she wouldn't want me walking through the house covered in skunk.

"Mom . . ."

She finally opened the door. "What? What's wrong?" Then the odor hit her. "Oh, Junior. Did you get sprayed by a skunk? Oh, my goodness." She waved her hand in front of her nose and turned her head. She closed the screen door and wouldn't let me come into the house.

"How did this happen? Where?" she asked.

There was nothing to do but to tell her the whole story.

"Serves you right," she said. "I've told you not to go down near the tracks. Good enough for you."

Then she started laughing, too.

"Mom . . ." This was awful. Here I was smelling like a skunk, my own mother's laughing at me, and she won't let me in the house.

"Well, I suppose the only thing to do is try the tomato-juice remedy. That's what they use when dogs get sprayed."

"Does it work?"

"Well, it's worth a try."

Mom took some money out of the change jar she kept in the kitchen. She opened the door and stuck her hand out.

"Here, go to Chip's—no, he won't have any

tomato juice. You'll have to go down to Borden's Market. Get a couple of big cans of tomato juice."

"But, Mom—I smell terrible. I can't go down there like this."

"I'm certainly not going. You're the one who disobeyed. You suffer the consequences. Here," she said, shoving the money at me.

There was no way out of this. I took the money and headed to Borden's. Let me tell you, I was not a welcome customer. Anyone who made the mistake of coming near me backed away quickly, covering his nose. And at the checkout there was no thank-you-come-again for me.

Mom made me strip down to my underwear in the backyard before she'd let me inside the house.

"And tiptoe upstairs to the bathroom," she warned.

She made me sit in the tub, as she poured water and tomato juice over me.

"What about this?" I asked, holding up my prized Red Sox cap.

"Well, we'll do the best we can."

Then I had to take a regular bath and wash my hat with strong soap.

"Mom, please don't tell Dad about this." I couldn't stand for him to know I had done something this stupid. I couldn't stand for him to know about the baseball hat.

"Well, he just might find out for himself."

I put my hat on the steps in the sun to dry.

"I don't know," Mom said, sniffing me. "I can still smell skunk."

"What am I going to do?" I asked.

Mom shook her head. "Let's just hope you fade by tomorrow. We're having people over to our party."

I took another bath before my dad came home from work. I even used some of Linda's talcum powder, Sweet Lily-of-the-Valley.

Linda sniffed me suspiciously when she sat down for supper that night. "Well, you certainly smell pretty tonight. You haven't been messing with my perfume, have you?" she asked.

Chapter Sixteen

After we ate, Dad and I finished sprucing up the yard for the party the next day.

"That about does it," Dad said, admiring the newly mown lawn. "Clean the mower off and put it back in the basement. And hurry up. It's getting dark."

"Okay." Dad was in a good mood. He was looking forward to using the new barbecue tomorrow.

I picked up the rake and held it under my arm. Then I rolled the lawn mower through the open bulkhead and down the cellar stairs. It was hard to balance. I felt the rake slipping, but the mower was pulling me forward. I couldn't stop.

Suddenly the rake hit the wall. I was really on my way down now! I fell sideways and put my arms out to catch myself.

Thump! Thump! Crash! The rake did a cartwheel down the stairs, and the lawn mower chased after it.

Crash! It was too dark to see, but I could hear something spinning and then thudding to the floor. The cellar light went on.

"What in the world is going on? What happened down here?" Dad hollered. "My lawn mower! And look at this mess!"

I limped down the stairs. Not only had the mower lost a wheel but it had crashed into a stack of boxes. There was stuff all over the floor—papers, picture albums, news clippings. Stuff I'd never known was down there.

Dad pushed the mower aside and knelt by the spilled boxes.

"I'm sorry, Dad. I'll clean it up," I said. "Please don't start yelling."

I started to gather up the papers and the albums. Several photographs slipped out.

"Leave it!" Dad ordered. "I'll do it!" He frantically began sweeping it all together with his hands.

I tried to help. I picked up a picture, and a face looked up at me. It was my dad's face. A young face. A young Dad wearing a leather flight jacket. He was kneeling with a group of men in front of a plane. They were looking at a map.

"Dad, it's you!" I said.

"Put it down! Leave this stuff alone! I told your mother to get rid of it years ago!"

"Dad, it's you when you were in the army." My eyes burned with excitement.

Dad took the picture from my hand. He looked at his own face in the photograph. He covered his eyes with his hand and sighed.

"Dad?" I said. I patted his arm. "Dad . . ."

He took his hand from his eyes and looked at the picture again and shook his head sadly. "My army buddies," he said. "There's Mike, and there's Don. And Ray!" Ray made him smile. "Ray was a real character." Dad sighed again. "And there's Paul. My best pal."

Wow! Dad had a best pal, like I had Lenny!

"We had some good times back then, in spite of it all. We stuck together. Looked out for each other."

"Do they live around here?" I asked. "How come you never see them? Go places with them?"

"Well, Mike is married. Last I heard he was living somewhere in Hawaii. Owned a pineapple plantation. Ray's married, too. Went back to Texas to work in his family's oil company. I don't know what's become of Don. I think he went on to college. We lost touch."

Wow! My dad had friends who lived in Hawaii and Texas!

"And what about your best pal, Paul?" I asked.

Dad tucked the photo back into the scrapbook.

"Dad? What about Paul?"

"Paul. One day . . ." Dad began. Then he looked away. "One day our plane was shot down, and Paul—well, Paul didn't make it. Paul died."

"Gee, Dad." I didn't know what to say. I hadn't been expecting that.

My dad cleared his throat, and then he wiped his nose.

"I'm sorry about your friend, Dad."

Then my eyes fell on a little hinged box on the floor.

"What's this?" I asked. I looked inside. There it was—the Silver Star. The medal I had heard so much about.

"Wow—the Silver Star!" I said. "You did something important, Dad. The Silver Star means you're a hero. Tell me!"

Dad looked down at it.

"I did my job. That's all. I got it for helping out," he said.

Then he picked up the Silver Star and held it in his hand like he was weighing it.

"Every man in the war was a hero. Every soldier was right there to help a buddy, even when he was scared himself. I'll tell you, I've seen some real courage. And that's what courage is about, Junior. Feeling scared and doing something to help anyway. We all did that in the war. That's how it was."

Dad covered his eyes again. "Oh, God! These pictures, this medal. It's like I'm right back there." Then he started crying.

Maybe the story was too hurtful for him to ever talk about. Maybe I shouldn't have asked. Then Dad surprised me.

"Our plane was shot down. It sliced the tops off a few trees before it crashed in a field and then broke apart. When I crawled out of the wreck, I was all alone. My arm and my knee were hurting pretty bad, but I was still able to walk. Then I spotted Mike and Ray. They were both unconscious, and I dragged them away from the wreck. Next I found Don. His leg was broken, and I helped him over to the others. Then I heard Paul. 'Somebody help me out of here!' he called. 'I'm trapped in here!' 'Coming, buddy! Hang on!' I called back. But before I could go back for Paul—"

Dad sobbed.

"It's okay, Dad. You don't have to tell the rest. It's okay," I said.

Dad looked up at me, and the tears streamed down his cheeks. "Before I could go back for Paul, my best friend in the world, the plane exploded. A huge fireball. I never made it back for Paul. And it's been so hard for me to get past that moment. Still trying to till this very day. I hope he knows. I hope he knows I wanted to save him."

I put my arm around my dad and gave him a hug.

"And then . . . and then when I was in the army hospital with a broken arm and a twisted knee, the next thing I knew my commanding officer was handing me this Silver Star. Telling me how brave I was. War is not a good thing, Junior. Yes, I'm proud that I helped our country in

World War II. I'm proud that I served in the Army Air Corps. But war is terrible, Junior. It hurts people in so many ways. And it never stops hurting, even after the war ends."

Then Dad put the Silver Star in my hand. I held it like I was weighing it.

Chapter Seventeen

I guess my favorite part of the Fourth of July parade was the fire trucks at the end. The sirens blared, and the firemen on the tanker would squirt water at us. The women would shriek and jump back from the curb. If you were one of the lucky kids, you'd get soaked.

I walked down Grove Street with my dad. This was the first time Dad had ever come with us to the parade.

"You're sure about this, Joe? You're going to be all right?" Mom asked.

"I'm sure. It's time I let the past be the past and get on with things. Don't you think?" he said, giving her a hug.

My mom and Linda and her friend Rita strolled behind us. The parade route would pass by the end of our street, right by the mill. Too bad Lenny was going to miss the parade this year. He had appointments with his doctors in Boston this week, and he and his parents drove up this morning to settle in. Lenny said his parents also had some sort of business to attend to.

We waited impatiently at our usual parade spot in front of Bobby's house. Bobby and his mother joined us under the tree.

"Dad, do you think we're going to have another war?" I asked. "Are the Communists coming here?"

"What in the world would make you ask questions like that?"

In school last year we had air-raid drills. We had to crawl under our desks and cover our faces. Miss Kane said we had to be ready in case anyone dropped bombs on us. It wasn't likely, she said, but we had to be ready.

"The news reporters on TV were talking about Communists," I said.

Dad put his arm around me. "Don't worry about things you hear on the news. People like to talk."

"I heard President Eisenhower talking about Communists, too."

"Junior, nobody in this country wants another war. Two world wars were enough. It's time to grow as a country. Time for people to come together to do good things for our nation. For the whole world."

I thought about Dad's friend Paul, who didn't get to see all the good things that were happening in our country.

"You won't ever have to go into the army again, will you, Dad?" I asked.

Dad laughed. "No, Uncle Sam wouldn't want an old man like me."

"You're not that old, Dad."

He pulled my Red Sox cap down over my eyes. He smiled, and then he sniffed.

"What's that smell?"

I yanked my hat off and stuffed it into my pocket.

"Here they come!" Linda said.

The high-school band was leading the parade. Linda and Rita called out and waved to some of their friends who hadn't graduated yet. A Brownie troop marched by.

"How cute," Mom said.

They were followed by the members of one of the new Little League teams that had started up this spring. Some carried bats. Some carried gloves. It was their blue-and-white-striped uniforms that caught my eye.

"Dad, will you sign me up for Little League next spring?" I asked.

"Sure will," he answered. "Wait till they see your pitch. Maybe I'll volunteer to coach."

"Really? You really will? That would be great, Dad."

Dad smiled. "Why not!"

There were the usual funny homemade floats. The mayor rode by in a fancy new convertible. There were tap dancers and baton twirlers. We could hear the loud cheers and applause as the group of marching veterans approached. Some men and boys whistled. I looked up at my dad. Please be all right, Dad, I thought.

Right in front of us. The flag bearer was passing right in front of us. And there was my dad standing tall, giving a snappy Air Corps salute. My heart drummed, and goose bumps galloped up and down my spine. Everything would be all right. I knew it now. Mom smiled at me and slipped her arm through Dad's.

Aoooogah! A horn blared. Next, some antique cars rolled past.

"Look! Look! It's Nancy!" Bobby said.

Aoooogah!

"That must be her grandfather's car," Mom said. "Nancy's mother was telling me about it."

There was Nancy sitting in the rumble seat, tossing chocolate kisses and butterscotch candies to the crowd. I hoped she wouldn't spot me.

"Hi, Junior!" she called, waving. She tossed a big handful of candy at me.

Bobby ran into the road with some little kids to pick up the candies. He handed me a couple of the chocolate kisses.

"No, you keep them," I said.

Sirens! The fire engines! The water truck!

"Right here! Right here!" kids yelled.

Shucks! I wasn't one of the lucky ones to get drenched. Well, maybe it was for the best—to keep my hat dry.

Mrs. Witowicz, Mrs. Stefanski, and Buster were waiting for us back at our house. Mom had invited them to our Fourth of July party. Both ladies had brought platters of Polish food. Dad got busy lighting the fire in the new barbecue pit.

"Go help your mother," he told me. "And keep that dog away from the food."

On the way into the house, I passed Bobby carrying out a tray of hamburger buns. There was so much chatter and clatter in the yard that Mom didn't hear me come into the kitchen. She was talking to Bobby's mother.

"Did you hear the news about Lenny?" Bobby's mother asked her.

"Yes, I did," Mom said.

"What news?" I asked.

Mom rolled her eyes at Bobby's mother, and she handed me some paper napkins and paper plates. "Take these outside. Go on. Out!"

The screen door slapped shut behind me.

What news about Lenny?

★ ---

Chapter Eighteen

Well, whatever Lenny's news was, it couldn't have been too important. When he got back from Boston he filled us in on all the sightseeing he'd done. He'd been to Faneuil Hall, toured Paul Revere's house, and driven right by Fenway Park, home of the Red Sox!

On the trip back home from Boston, Lenny had done some thinking about how we could earn more money these last couple of weeks of summer. We had managed to make a few dollars washing windows at Chip's store, but there still wasn't enough for a bike or a raft.

"Kool-Aid," Lenny said. "We'll sell Kool-Aid. We could make a lot of money with a Kool-Aid stand on a hot day," he said.

Lenny's mother donated the Kool-Aid, and I got the ice, the Tupperware pitcher, the paper cups, and the TV-tray tables from my house. Dad helped me carry some of the stuff outside before he left for work.

"Hi, Bobby! Hi, Lenny!" he said, patting Lenny on the back. "You boys save some Kool-Aid for me when I come home."

Lenny stiffened out of habit. "I can't believe your dad is being so friendly to me lately," he whispered. "He's sure been acting different. I don't get it."

I shrugged. Dad was probably thinking more about friends these days. Maybe he was starting to understand how I felt about Lenny. Anyway, it didn't feel right to tell Lenny the story about Dad's Silver Star. It was Dad's story. He would tell it himself when he was ready.

My friends and I got busy setting everything up on the sidewalk near my front yard. Bobby was making the sign.

"What should we charge?" he asked.

"I think we'd better go with a nickel a cup," Lenny suggested.

"Just a nickel?" I asked. It didn't seem to me we were going to make much money selling Kool-Aid.

"That's the usual price."

The three of us made ourselves comfortable on our plastic lawn chairs, reading comics, and listening to the deejay on the transistor radio I borrowed—okay, took—from Linda's room. Business was starting off slow. Buster came over to keep us company. He plopped himself down beside my chair.

Finally, we had our first customer. Mrs. Witowicz came out to sit in her yard and spotted us. She waved and ambled over.

"Nice. You boychiks sell soda," she said, smiling.

"No, it's Kool-Aid," I said.

"Kool-Aid? What's that?" she asked.

"Kids like it," Bobby said.

"And grown-ups, too!" I added.

"Try some," Lenny said. "Five cents a cup."

Mrs. Witowicz reached into her apron pocket.

Uh-oh, I thought. Here comes something wrapped in waxed paper. But to my relief Mrs. Witowicz took out a nickel and plunked it into the empty can next to Bobby. A real nickel.

Mrs. Witowicz took a sip. "Good, good!" she said. "I like."

We sat there for another half hour or so. The

noon sun was beating down on the cement. I could smell the rubber on our sneakers melting. Buster panted, and his huge pink tongue lolled over his loose lips. Linda's batteries had run down, and the heat was making us cranky. We started arguing over the comics.

"I'll trade you the Superman for the Archie," Lenny said to me.

"What do you mean?" Bobby said. "That Superman is mine. You said you'd trade me a Batman for it!"

"Well, there wasn't actually a trade," Lenny said. "I told you I'd think about it."

"Hey, guys! Look!" I said.

There, right across the street from us, were Nancy and Ellen setting up a Kool-Aid stand in the shade. They smiled and waved.

"What do they think they're doing!" Lenny said.

"Yeah, this is our idea!" I said.

"Copycats!" Lenny yelled to them.

Nancy stuck out her tongue.

"Look at their sign!" Bobby said. " 'Kool-Aid and a Cookie—5 Cents.' "

"Hey!" Lenny said.

"Hey!" I said.

Then along came the mailman on his morning route.

"Well, look at this! Just what I need—a cold drink and a cookie, too!" He handed over a nickel and walked on.

Now I was standing with my hands on my hips. I was really mad!

"This isn't fair!" I said. "Can you get some cookies from your mom?" I asked Lenny.

"Are you kidding? I had to beg for the Kool-Aid. How about you?" Lenny asked me.

"No, my mom put Dad on a diet, and we don't even have a Ritz cracker in the pantry."

"Don't look at me," Bobby said.

"Great!" I complained. "Now look!"

There was the milkman buying a drink—and a cookie—from Nancy.

"I guess we picked the wrong spot," Lenny said. "Everyone would rather walk on the shady side of the street."

"Yeah."

"Yeah," Bobby said, licking his lips. "I think we should have a sip of our Kool-Aid to cheer us up."

"Well, a half cup each wouldn't hurt," I said. It was very hot in the sun.

Lenny poured a small cup for each of us. We

gulped them right down. Poor Buster was staring at us and whining. Lenny poured some Kool-
Aid into my cupped hands, and Buster lapped it
up. It wasn't nearly enough to quench our thirst.

"How about another cup?" Bobby asked.

"Why not?" Lenny said, pouring more.

We sat there drinking our pitcher of Kool-Aid
and fuming at the girls.

"A cookie sure would be good right about
now," Bobby said, drumming the table with his
fingers.

Then, before Lenny or I knew what was happening, Bobby reached right into the money can
and grabbed our one and only nickel. In a flash
he was across the street, buying Kool-Aid and a
cookie from the girls.

"Traitor! Traitor!" Lenny called.

Bobby came back to our stand and handed
me a cookie. "Nancy said this is for you."

There was Nancy smiling over at me. I broke
the cookie and gave a piece to Buster and a
piece to Lenny.

"Thanks, Nancy!" Lenny taunted.

Nancy shook her fist.

Chapter Nineteen

It was hard to face the truth. My vacation was nearly over, and I knew I would never have a bike that summer. For all the plans I'd made and all the work I'd done, I had just about nothing to show for it. I'd managed to stash away some of my allowance, and I still had the Christmas money I'd saved up, but it wasn't enough for a bike. I'd just have to wait until my birthday in October, like Dad said.

Lenny and Bobby were definitely getting the rubber raft they'd seen at Jim & Harry's Hardware Store. I decided to add my money to theirs and go in on the raft, too.

We kept the raft in Lenny's backyard, leaning against the side of his house. The three of us would lug it down to the pond and row around all afternoon. We were the only kids in the neighborhood who had a raft, so it attracted a lot of attention.

One afternoon at the pond we met up with Ricky. He was hanging out alone, whittling a branch with that boot knife of his.

"Hey, there's Huey, Dewey, and Louie gonna float in their little toy boat," Ricky jeered. "Ain't youse supposed to be swimmin'? Quack! Quack!" How he laughed at his own stupid joke!

We set down the raft, and then we walked around the edge of the pond a bit, watching for minnows and water bugs. Nancy and Ellen came along and started bothering us. So we helped Lenny push the raft into the water, and then Bobby and I walked down to a quieter spot to fish. I got lucky and felt a strong pull on my line. I reeled in a good-size bass. I was just about to call out to brag to Lenny, who had been drifting in the raft. Suddenly I heard him yelling.

"The boat's leaking! I'm sinking!" He was frantically using both hands to scoop out the water.

Before I leaped into the pond, I spotted Ricky lurking behind the trees onshore.

Bobby and I swam out to the raft and reached it just as it sank. Lenny took a dunking and went limp. Bobby and I half dragged and half carried him out of the water. We laid him on the grass, and Bobby ran for help.

"Help! We need help!" I yelled.

A group of kids gathered around. I tried to remember how to do that artificial-respiration stuff.

"Do something! Do something!" Nancy screamed at me.

"But I don't know what to do!" I said. I slapped Lenny's face a couple of times, and I thought I saw him wince.

"Talk to me, Lenny! Say something! Somebody, help us!" I yelled.

"He's dead! He's dead!" Nancy screamed.

Ricky came running out of the woods and knelt beside Lenny. "Hey, kid, are you okay?" he said. His eyes were popping out of his head, and he looked as white as a frog's belly. He shook Lenny a few times. "Hey, kid! Wake up!"

I got up and stood out of the way, glad to have help from someone—even if it was Ricky.

"Kid, answer me!" Ricky pleaded.

There was no warning. Without a flutter of an eye or a twitch of a hand, Lenny leaped up and yelled right in Ricky's face, "BOO!"

Ricky jumped up on woobly legs and clutched his shaking arms. Lenny made us all jump. I didn't know whether to laugh or cry.

Bobby came back with Dr. Lewis. They raced over to us. The crowd of onlookers parted to let Dr. Lewis through.

"Are you all right, Lenny?" Dr. Lewis asked.

"He was dead, Daddy! He was dead and he came back to life!" Nancy screeched.

"Oh, Nancy! For heaven's sake!" her father said.

Lenny sat there grinning and wringing out his T-shirt.

"Yeah, I'm okay," he said.

I turned to look at Ricky. He was backing away, and then he ran off into the woods.

"I'm okay," Lenny said.

✳ ✳ ✳

Well, the raft was ruined. Something had punctured it. A branch? A knife? Dad patched it and made it float. But it never felt safe, especially with Ricky lurking around. I didn't trust it in the water again. Besides, the summer was coming to an end, and we wouldn't have much time left for the raft anyway.

Chapter Twenty

The cereal box. I was reading the back of the cereal box when I heard the first fire engine wail. I jumped up and ran to the door.

"Junior, sit down and eat your breakfast," Mom said, steering me back to the table.

"Oh, Mom! I'll finish it later," I said.

"Sit!"

The screen door flew open. Lenny burst into the kitchen.

"Junior! Mrs. Webster! The mill's on fire! The Mansfield-Davis is on fire!"

"Oh, my God!" Mom screamed. "Your father! Linda!" She threw down her dish towel and raced out of the house, curlers still in her hair.

I ran after her, and Lenny followed as fast as he could.

Dad and Linda had started their shift an hour ago. My dad and my sister!

Another fire truck sped by. Then another. I heard more sirens in the distance. The clamor was bringing everyone out into their yards, into the street. People were running toward the mill.

My mother and I stood across from the mill. A huge crowd continued to gather. Mom had her hands to her face, crying.

"Joe! Linda! Oh, where are they?" she said.

Lenny and Bobby joined us on the corner.

"Did your father get out okay?" Bobby asked.

"Shut up! Shut up!" I hollered. I didn't want to think of Dad and Linda in that burning mill.

There was a shriek from the crowd as the mill's roof caved in. Everyone moved back from the curb. My mother screamed, and I hid my face in her housecoat. Sparks shot out everywhere. Then came the explosion.

"Move back! Move back!" the policemen ordered. Babies were crying, and people were yelling to each other.

Mom grabbed a policeman's arm. "My daughter! My husband! They both work here!" she said. "Did the workers get out? Is everyone out?"

"Ma'am. I don't have much information," he said. "But, yes, most of the people made it out safely."

My mom pushed through the crowd, searching and calling. We bumped into the mill workers who had made it out in time. Many were covered with soot. They were coughing, and many were sobbing. We couldn't find my father or sister anywhere.

"Mom, let's go home," I said. "Maybe Dad and Linda are there."

"No! No! They're here somewhere! I know it! I've got to find them! Joe? Linda? Oh, God!"

A man reached out for Mom's shoulder and spun her around.

"Carol, we're okay! We're okay!"

I hardly recognized him. It was my dad! His face was covered with grime except for the white rings around his eyes. And Linda was right by his side. We all hugged, and I bawled louder than any baby there.

"Watch out! Watch out!" a policeman said, herding people away from the blazing mill. A fireball shot up into the air, and burning embers landed close to some of the nearby houses.

"That's all we need," Dad said. "Houses catching on fire."

More fire engines came. More police and rescue trucks came. The firemen hosed down the houses near the mill so they wouldn't catch on fire.

Parts of the burning mill were flying everywhere, landing in people's yards. A flaming hunk of wood landed right on Bobby's house.

Lenny was bellowing, "Bobby! Bobby! Stay here! Bobby!"

We turned to look, and there was Bobby racing into his house.

"What is he doing!" my dad exclaimed. My father ran after him. "Bobby!"

Then Bobby appeared on his second-floor porch. He looked like a wild man up there.

"He's trying to save his bike!" I said.

Bobby picked up his Junior Police Raleigh and tossed it down to the street from two stories up. It hit the road with a bounce and then bounced again and flipped over once, twice. The front wheel and the handlebars broke off.

"There's a kid up there!" someone shouted.

"Jump! Jump!" someone else yelled.

"No! No! Stay there! I'm coming!" my dad called.

He pushed his way through the crowd and stood right below Bobby. "Don't move!"

Then Dad shinnied up the porch post. "Give me your hand! Climb on my back!"

"They'll both be killed!" my mother cried.

Lenny dashed into the middle of the road, waving his arms wildly. The ladder truck barreling down the street blared its horn, and the firemen on board motioned Lenny out of the way.

"The house is on fire! The house is on fire!" Lenny shouted.

The truck stopped inches away from Lenny. "There's a kid up there!" Lenny said, pointing to the porch.

The firemen worked furiously to get the ladder into place. The third floor of Bobby's tenement was disappearing in flames.

Dad said something to Bobby, and Bobby shook his head. Bobby's feet seemed welded to the porch. Dad climbed onto the burning porch with him.

The crowd gasped.

Dad pulled Bobby onto his back and slid back down the porch post.

The firemen and the crowd clapped and

cheered. A hose truck came and put out the fire, but it was obvious that no one would be calling that place home ever again.

We walked over to where Bobby's bike lay in pieces on the ground. Bobby knelt down and held the handlebars in his lap.

✳ ✳ ✳

The mill burned all day. Seven communities sent equipment to help put out the fire. Pictures of the Mansfield-Davis, or, rather, the rubble that was left, filled the newspapers. Reporters talked about the mill on TV, too.

We were watching the news on television that night when the doorbell rang. It was Lenny's father.

"Tom! Come on in," Dad said.

"Joe. Hello," Lenny's father said, stepping inside. "Well, I know we haven't been on the best of terms. We've had words. But I came here to tell you what a fine thing you did today—saving Bobby's life. You're a brave man."

"Please," Dad said. "You would have done the same thing."

"To be honest with you, Joe, I'm not so sure. I don't know if I would have kept my wits about me. I just wanted to shake your hand, and say I'm proud to know you."

He reached out his hand.

Dad stood staring down at the rug. He shook his head no.

"Joe . . ." Mom said, nudging him.

"No," Dad said. "I'm not the brave one. Your son is the brave one. Running into the street like that. Stopping the fire truck. That took courage. I want to shake your hand. I'm proud to know your son."

And Dad reached out his hand.

✳ ✳ ✳

A week later a police car parked in front of Ricky's house. Neighbors gathered outside.

"I wonder . . ." Dad said, pushing open the screen door.

"Joe! Don't you go out there! That's none of our business!" Mom said.

"Well, it sure is! There's a police car on our street, and I need to know what's going on!"

I tried to skip out the door behind Dad.

"Oh, no, you don't!" Mom said, grabbing my shirt.

People were standing around gossiping. The

police were questioning Ricky about the fire. Some people were saying Ricky had started it. Someone claimed to have seen him around the mill acting suspiciously.

To everyone's surprise, the police left alone —without Ricky. People talked about Ricky for weeks, but no one could prove anything.

Linda said, "I know Ricky pretty well from high school. I hate to say it, but it's possible he did have something to do with the fire."

"Keep your thoughts to yourself. You don't know anything for sure," Mom said.

"Well, I think he started that fire!" I said. "He'd do something like that!"

"Junior!" Mom said, giving me a stern look.

"I'm with Junior," Dad said.

I guess Ricky was lying low. We didn't see him around for a while.

And Bobby's bike? Pete worked on it at his garage. For free. He got it looking as good as new. Well, almost. Every now and then Bobby had to take it back over there so Pete could readjust the wheel.

Chapter Twenty-one

Lenny's news. I couldn't believe it—didn't want to believe it. Lenny sure laid a heavy one on me when he told me he was moving. He'd only found out about it himself that week. Just before school started, he and his family moved to Boston, where Lenny could be close to his doctors.

"We'll write letters," Lenny suggested. "You can tell me everything about sixth grade, and let me know when you try out for Little League."

It would take me a long time to get over saying goodbye to Lenny. If I ever got over it at all. This time both of us had tears burning red in our eyes. He climbed into the back seat of his family's car, and it was over just like that. He waved to me from the window, and I waved back. Then he was gone.

Lenny's mother called to say his doctors were hopeful that in a couple of years he wouldn't need the leg brace anymore. That was good news, but I sure missed him a lot. Without Lenny nothing would ever be the same. He always had the best ideas, the best questions, and the best answers.

Lenny wrote me a letter about his new school. He said it was a lot bigger than Grove Street School. His new teacher was going to be Mr. Seymour Beans. I laughed till I cried. Lenny's new friend was a neighbor named Charlie. I felt jealous when he told me about him, but I knew that Lenny needed a friend as much as I needed Bobby.

Seeing how down in the dumps I was, Dad tried to cheer me up. He bought me a bike a whole month before my birthday, even though we were short on money since the mill burned down.

"We'll take a trip to visit Lenny next summer," Dad said. "There's a great amusement park up his way. We'll take Bobby, too."

After the mill fire, Bobby and his mother moved right across the street from me, to the second floor of Mrs. Stefanski's house.

"You'll take me to see Lenny?" I asked. "Really?" Dad had sure changed his mind about polio.

"Yeah, sure! I'll never forget how Lenny stopped that fire truck in front of Bobby's burning house. What a kid! Yeah, we'll go see Lenny!"

Every now and then I'd bring out that photo I'd saved. The one that appeared on the front page of the newspaper—the photo of Dad climbing down Bobby's porch with Bobby on his back. Hero! That's what the reporter called Dad.

"Hero?" Dad would say. "Lenny is the hero."

✳ ✳ ✳

After the Mansfield-Davis Mill burned down, a lot of people were out of work. Dad was lucky, though. He got a new job at Bowen's Spinning. Linda's friend Rita got her a job at the bank, as secretary to the car-loan manager. One day Linda's old boyfriend Roger came in, wanting a loan for a new car.

"When Roger walked in, he looked right at me and pretended he didn't even know me," Linda said. "Huh!"

Linda's boss shook his head, as Roger left empty-handed.

"I hated to say no, but how can I give him a loan?" her boss said. "His last car was repossessed, and he makes peanuts at the bowling alley."

When fall came, Mrs. Witowicz sold her house and moved in with her friend Mrs. Stefanski in the first-floor apartment. Bobby said they played polka music on the radio day and night.

One day when Mom was reading the newspaper I heard her exclaim, "Well, look at this! Would you just look! Wait till your father sees this!"

"What?" I said, peering over her shoulder.

"Look! It's Ricky!"

There was a picture of Ricky wearing an army uniform and a little article about him completing basic training.

"Are you sure it's him?" I asked.

"Yes, that's him—Richard Franklin Rondo."

"Franklin?"

"I guess he was named after Franklin Roosevelt," Mom said.

I looked again. It was hard to tell it was Ricky. He sure did look different. He was wearing a cap, but I could still tell that all his hair had been shaved off. So that's where he'd been all these weeks—in the army. He did have plans after all.

That got me thinking how Mom had been right about a lot of things. It seemed I was doing a lot of thinking lately.

"Mom, how do you know if things are working out the way they should? How do you know for sure if you're headed in the right direction?"

Mom sighed. "Wish I knew the answer to that one. Haven't figured it out yet myself. You just have to trust yourself to make the best decisions you can. Deciding what's the responsible thing to do, what feels right for you." Then she smiled. "And sometimes, honey, life is mysterious. Life has a way of getting you where you're supposed to be."

✻ ✻ ✻

The first day of the new school year, Bobby stopped by so we could go together.

"Wait!" Mom called. She had my bow tie in her hand.

"Mom, not the bow tie. Nobody in the sixth grade wears a bow tie the first day of school," I said.

And this time she didn't insist.

Dad was on his way to work.

"Well, look at you all slicked up," he said. "Looking all grown-up."

I smiled at Mom. "Getting there," I said.

"Junior, are you coming or what?" Bobby called. He pushed the kickstand up and swung his leg over the bar of his bike. "The first bell will be ringing soon."

But it sounded like "winging."

I jumped on my bike and rode off to sixth grade with Buster chasing after me. It was hard to believe school was starting again. I could feel the shimmer of summer lingering in the air. I was racing to school past Mrs. Witowicz and Mrs. Stefanski chatting in the yard, past Nancy taunting us with Kool-Aid and cookies, past Richard Franklin Rondo loafing on the corner. Racing past memories of summer. Racing past my dad saluting the American flag at the Fourth of July parade. Racing past Lenny in the middle of the road waving down the fire truck. Racing past heroes.